MW01223734

GONE SOUTH

GONE SOUTH

and Other Ways to Disappear

JULIA LEGGETT

short stories

Mother Tongue Publishing Limited
Salt Spring Island, BC
Canada

MOTHER TONGUE PUBLISHING LIMITED
290 Fulford-Ganges Road, Salt Spring Island, B.C. V8K 2K6 CANADA
www.mothertonguepublishing.com
Represented in North America by Heritage Group Distribution.

Gone South is a work of fiction. Names, characters, places, and incidents are the
products of the author's imagination or are used fictitiously. Any resemblance to
actual events, locales, or persons, living or dead, is entirely coincidental.

Book Design by Mark Hand
Front landscape photo © Monika Gniot/Shutterstock
Typefaces used are Bodoni and Simplifica.

Printed on Enviro Cream, 100% recycled
Printed and bound in Canada.

Mother Tongue Publishing gratefully acknowledges the assistance of the Province of British
Columbia through the B.C. Arts Council and we acknowledge the support of the Canada Council
for the Arts, which last year invested $157 million in writing and publishing throughout Canada.
Nous remercions de son soutien le Conseil des Arts du Canada, qui a investi
157$ millions de dollars l'an dernier dans les lettres et l'édition à travers le Canada.

LIBRARY AND ARCHIVES CANADA
CATALOGUING IN PUBLICATION

Leggett, Julia, 1982-, author
        Gone south and other ways to disappear : short
stories / Julia Leggett.

ISBN 978-1-896949-39-0 (pbk.)

        I. Title.

PS8623.E46673G66 2014   C813'.6   C2014-904848-3

For my parents,
Sylvia and John

Contents

In Disguise

This was the first time Isabel had joined Tom on one of his work trips to Italy. He'd asked her to come every time, but she preferred having the house in London to herself and he knew it. She felt liberated to be away from him. Her life became disordered, mysterious. Tom liked tidiness and routine. Without him, Isabel let the washing-up grow filmy in the sink. She dropped her coat and bag on the floor and kicked her shoes off in the hallway. She drank gin and ate almonds in bed. She was glad he went away, but she was glad, too, when he came home. The books went back on the shelves in their rightful places. The bills were paid on time. With Tom she didn't have to worry if she let the menial tasks slide. He took care of things. He was her buffer.

But this time when he'd asked her along, she was sitting at the breakfast table reading an article on Berlusconi. In the photograph, Rome resembled a honeycomb, lit up in afternoon light. Isabel looked out the window into the garden; the rain fell steadily, and beneath the yew tree, chairs huddled together like ponies in a field. She pressed her fingertips against the glossy page, leaving little smudges.

"It might be nice to get away for a bit," she said.

Tom tried to disguise his surprise. "Great," he said. "Great."

Tom and Alessandra were turned away from her, discussing a mutual colleague. Isabel stared openly at Alessandra's profile. Alessandra was small with thick, dark curly hair. Her clothes were plain but arresting. Her white cotton shirt could have been a designer dress. Isabel felt outsized, ungainly. How did some women achieve that effortless chic? Isabel's clothes collected stray hairs and cake crumbs and grew stained at the cuffs. Isabel hadn't really given any thought to Alessandra before. She was simply *that professor* of English at the University of Rome, co-writing the *Introduction to English Literature* reader with Tom. Alessandra had existed on the periphery of Isabel's world. But here, in the piazza of the Pantheon, she shifted into full focus. Her golden skin. Her full and coral-coloured lips.

"I know!" Alessandra threw her hands up. Her eyes glittered. "He's always telling me the same thing, that he doesn't have time to write articles because he is so busy teaching, but really he's sleeping in his office." Her English was grammatically perfect but still accented. It made everything she said sound vaguely erotic. Tom laughed in his clipped, stilted way.

Alessandra smiled at Isabel. "Oh, but this is probably boring for you, Isabel, us crusty academics sharing unfunny jokes." She pointed up at the Pantheon's facade. "See the writing? It reads Marcus Agrippa, son of Lucius, built this."

Isabel tipped her head back and looked up. Inside her coat pockets, her hands were clenched.

"Only he didn't build it." Tom turned towards Alessandra. "At least not this one. Talk about stealing Hadrian's thunder." They both laughed.

"There's water on your glasses, Tom," Isabel said, pointing at him. Raindrops speckled the left lens, and behind it, his eye looked weak and rheumy. Tom removed his glasses and wiped each lens with the bottom of his navy blue fleece.

Tom and Isabel had been married for ten years. They had met in university. They'd both worked for the uni paper. He'd always paused at her desk to talk about current affairs, both of them regurgitating other people's opinions. He was jocular. He'd given her a nickname, Mousy Issy, and offered to make her cups of tea or get her packets of crisps from the vending machine on the third floor. He looked at her too long. At night when the office closed, he walked her to the bus stop. His advances were so clichéd that Isabel felt the tiniest bit repulsed. Still, at the staff Christmas party, after five gin and tonics and a snakebite, she ended up with him in the paper supply cupboard. The sex had been awkward. Isabel was a virgin, but she only told him afterwards as they lay in a little puddle of cum and blood, among a fluttering of A4 sheets of paper.

They continued to see each other after that. She never thought of it as a decision. She simply unfurled into him. Their match surprised the rest of the editorial staff. Once Isabel overheard Mark, the sports columnist, in the hallway outside the men's room asking Tom if Isabel's dreamy nature didn't drive him insane.

"I couldn't handle it," Mark said. "She's only ever half present. She's so drippy. I'm always stunned at how good she is at her work."

"Actually, I find it endearing."

Isabel, out of sight, standing two feet away in the doorway of the photocopying room, smiled. She, too, liked that they had opposing natures. Tom ploughed into life; she floated behind, carried along by his wash.

The wind lassoed Isabel's scarf from her neck and blew it across the piazza, where it wrapped around the legs of a dark-haired man in a leather jacket, who stood with his back to them. He turned and looked down at his legs in surprise, and then he pulled the scarf loose.

"Questa appartiene a voi?" he called out to them, the scarf held out in his hand like a red bouquet.

"Si, grazie." Alessandra went forward to collect it from him, but Isabel intercepted her.

"It's mine," she said to the man, her hand closing on it. The loop of the scarf connected them both, a thin red cord like a vein. The man released his end. With the tension gone, the scarf fluttered limply in the air. Isabel gathered it into her arms. The man nodded at her, his eyes dark, almost black.

"Grazie," Isabel said. Her cheeks flushed.

"Are you cold, Isabel?" Alessandra turned away from the man. "I know a wonderful espresso bar nearby." And she nodded at Isabel in the same professional way the Alitalia airhostess had when she'd placed the napkin and peanuts on Isabel's tray table.

The espresso bar was dark inside and full of working-class Italians in long winter coats. They stood up at the wooden bar, smoking cigarettes or picking at a pastry, drinking their coffee in flashes, like hummingbirds diving at a feeder.

"Isn't this authentic?" Tom's damp goatee bristled against Isabel's ear, and she shifted away from him.

"Tre cappuccini per favore?" Alessandra told the barman over the shrill of the espresso machine. She moved over to make space for them at the bar.

"So Isabel, Tom tells me you're a copy editor. That must be interesting work. I was actually thinking of pursuing journalism as an undergrad back when I was full of fire about the state of the world." Alessandra lifted her cup up halfway to her mouth and then returned it to its saucer and laughed, even though as far as Isabel could tell, she had not said anything funny. Her laugh gurgled, the sound of water going down the drain.

"There's not much fire involved in copy editing," Isabel said. "If I were going to use an element to describe it, I'd probably choose ice."

"Still Tom says you work for the *Guardian*. That's a major paper with some serious political clout."

"Mm." Isabel skimmed the foam of her cappuccino with the tip of her teaspoon.

Tom leaned forward between them to face Alessandra. "Isabel copy edits all of my work for me too, and quite frankly, she's outstanding at it."

"It's such a pity we already have a copy editor for our book," Alessandra said. "Otherwise you could have edited it, Isabel."

"I wouldn't have had the time." Isabel brought her cup up to her lips.

Tom put both his hands in his lap. He smiled vaguely, as though he were on a stage and the spotlight was blinding him and he couldn't tell who was in the crowd.

In the street, the three of them stood facing each other. The sun was setting, and in the distance, Isabel could see a flock of pigeons circling a pine tree, their bodies black cutouts against the wintry pink sky.

"Home for a rest? And then out for dinner at my local trattoria?" Alessandra did up her coat buttons. Her flesh-toned nail varnish made her fingers look vulnerable.

"Sounds perfect," Tom said in his jolly up voice. "Doesn't it Isabel?"

"The birds are roosting." Isabel drew out the oo sound as if she were sucking on a sweet. "How lovely."

"What?" The skin around Tom's lips whitened. This was their dance, he became jovial and practical, and she became vague and whimsical. They could never deal with something straight on.

"I said that would be lovely."

Alessandra and Tom strode ahead, and Isabel fell behind; she watched the evening darken around them. She liked how the fading light turned the terracotta buildings rosy, set them aglow. As they approached an intersection, Isabel stopped.

"Shit," she said. "I've left my scarf in the espresso bar."

Tom turned around. "We can go back. It's not that far."

Behind Alessandra, the traffic lights flashed amber and then red. The traffic stopped.

"I'll go back on my own; I know my way home from here. I'll catch up to you," Isabel said.

"Are you sure, darling? You're terrible with directions." Tom gave Alessandra a sideways look as though inviting her to partake.

Alessandra stepped towards the curb. "It's only six blocks from here. If you do get lost, you can get a map at any giornalaio." Her voice sounded so bright it made Isabel think of tin foil.

"It's not exactly backcountry orienteering, I'll be fine," Isabel said, and she laughed in a brittle way.

Tom said nothing. He turned back towards Alessandra. Behind him, the traffic began to move.

Isabel's scarf lay curled up on the floor underneath the bar like a sleepy red snake. The espresso bar was empty now. Everyone must already be at home yelling at their wives because dinner wasn't ready or in bed with their mistresses. The barman stared openly at her as she crossed the floor. He leaned over the wooden bar and watched her pick up the scarf. Straightening up, Isabel felt the soft friction of her skin against her clothes.

"I forgot it," she said. "Earlier." His expression didn't change. Isabel stood stiffly in front of him. "Arrivederci," she said. He turned his back on her.

Outside in the rain, most of the shops and cafes were dark, their shutters pulled down. Isabel walked quickly. She turned left into a narrow street, and came out into a piazza, facing the Pantheon. Isabel stopped, certain she had been walking in the opposite direction. She stood for a moment, the rain falling on her face, and then she moved under the shelter of the awning in front of McDonald's. If she thought this through carefully, she would be able to work it out. She'd just got a little disorientated. Once she knew where she was going, she could catch up with Tom and Alessandra. They wouldn't even have to know she'd got lost. In the window, her reflection had damp hair that fell flat against her face. Her mascara had smudged, and her open coat hung loosely about her. Two girls came through the glass doors of McDonald's arm in arm. They stared at her, doe-eyed with adolescence. Isabel shifted further away from the entrance. She scanned the piazza. A group of Japanese tourists were standing right where she had stood to look up at the engraving on the front of the Pantheon earlier that afternoon. Behind them, a street curved out from the corner of the piazza; Isabel thought it led back to Alessandra's apartment. She walked down the street about hundred metres. Nothing looked familiar. Alleyways shot off at odd angles. She stopped in front of a gelato store. The sign had two Raphaelesque baby angels on it licking ice cream cones. Their pink tongues were obscene. She would have remembered this. She turned back. It was dark now, and the fluorescent lighting of the McDonald's lit up the piazza. It gave everything a blasted, artificial feel. She would try to retrace her steps. She walked purposively towards the two narrow streets that exited on the left-hand side and then stopped. She didn't know which one she had come down.

Isabel ran her hand over her face. This was ridiculous. She had an urge to cry. She swung round. The Japanese tourists were leaving. A little distance behind them, preoccupied with something in his hands, stood the man with the leather jacket who had returned her scarf to her. His pronounced cheekbones and wide-set eyes gave him an arrogant look, but his smooth and honey-like skin softened him, made him almost boyish. He held a camera and stared down at it in a concentrated manner for a few more seconds and then slipped it into his jacket pocket. He looked up and right through her, and then he walked out of the piazza.

Isabel followed him.

In the station, the man stopped to buy a newspaper. Isabel looped around the newsagent stand, skirted the escalators and then swung back. In the international section, she picked up a copy of the *Guardian Weekly* and stood beside the rack of magazines. She hadn't really thought this through. The man seemed to be choosing between two papers. He turned them over and looked at the sports section. Isabel scanned the *Guardian*. The front page was a long piece on climate change she hadn't edited. There had been flooding in Norfolk. Nothing spectacular, no one rowing out of their homes or trapped on their roofs waving helplessly at helicopter crews. Just old couples up to their ankles, telling reporters that it had ruined their carpets. The article announced with authority that this was the wettest winter in Britain since 1963. Isabel was pleased someone was calibrating this, all of it. Winters seemed to come and go for her, wet and dry, without any real distinguishing features. She wondered sometimes if she were not simply stupid. She was so easily distracted. She looked up. The man tucked his newspaper under his arm and crossed the station forecourt to join a line at a ticket window. Isabel stood behind the magazine rack, watching, until a woman in a red coat and leopard-print stilettos joined the line, and then Isabel went and stood behind her.

"Ostia Antica," the man told the teller when he got to the front of the line, and then he said something Isabel couldn't understand in his raspy voice. She saw now that he was not as well-dressed as she had thought. He had missed a patch shaving, and he needed a haircut; a curl of thick hair fell messily over his ear, giving him an impish profile. He took his ticket and walked away. Isabel half-stepped out of the line. The woman in the red coat rested her hand up against the side of the teller's window and spoke rapidly. The man had reached the escalators, and Isabel felt a little quiver in her throat. The woman in the red coat drummed her hand twice against the wall, shook her head and walked away without buying a ticket. Isabel stepped up to the window.

"Ostia Antica, per favore?" she said, the decision made now.

The teller tried to tell her something, but she shook her head. "English."

The teller fell silent. He held her gaze as if he could intimidate her into understanding Italian, and then he made a snapping action with his fingers. He took her money and gave her a ticket. "Binario Cinque." His index finger banged against the Plexiglas.

Isabel ran across the forecourt. Her scarf, unloosened by the motion, slid from her shoulders and caught around her knees. She pulled it free and ran on with it hooked over her arms.

She boarded the last carriage of the train and walked slowly down the central aisle. She planned to walk the entire length of the train, but almost immediately she saw the man. She recognized the shape of his shoulders in his leather jacket. She slipped into an empty seat two rows behind him. She could see the corners of his paper on either side of his head. He was reading the world news. Afghanistan was in the headline. As the train pulled away from the station, Isabel suddenly felt afraid. What was she thinking? Tom would be so embarrassed; he hated any display of oddity. Don't be strange, he always told her. It would be better if she called him from the station at Ostia Antica pretending to be lost than told him the truth. If she told him she thought the way home to Alessandra's apartment included a forty-five minute train ride to another city, he probably wouldn't even be surprised. That way he could tell the story when they were back in London, and out for dinner with friends, everyone laughing at how scatterbrained she was and Tom touching her arm, and looking about him as though he was the proprietor of a purse-winning racehorse.

The train seat smelled of sweat and cigarettes. Isabel brought her wrist up to her nose and inhaled her own scent. The image of Alessandra in the profumeria at the piazza di Spagna flashed into Isabel's mind. The way she had uncorked the bottle of Chanel Coco Mademoiselle and dabbed. The way she held out her hand to Tom and he caught her elbow and lowered his face into the crook of her arm; his eyelashes glancing her skin. Isabel had seen the slightest tremor of pleasure lift at the corners of Alassandra's mouth.

Or Isabel could not phone Tom at all. She could disappear. She pictured Tom's panic. He would contact the police and file a missing persons report. A manhunt set in motion; thousands of carabinieri pouring into the streets, the thousands of red vertical stripes on their trousers flicking by. Isabel looked out the window as the train passed through the scrappy edges of the city. Parking lots and dumpsters, chain-link fences and abandoned cars. She could do anything. The railway line veered up to the highway, and the train zipped along with the Fiats and the Smart cars. Isabel felt calmer; she liked public transport, she liked the lack of responsibility. She had never learned to drive. Tom thought being able to drive set you free. He learned at seventeen "by bombing about the country lanes of Much Hadham like a lunatic." He always said this with admiration for his younger self. Tom thought of freedom in terms of will; the freedom to act, to be an agent, Isabel thought of it in negatives. In a train, you were not in the world; you simply moved past it, you were nowhere. As with space exploration, no tangible relationship to the landscape existed—in your regulated capsule, you stared out in wonder at the mysterious alien planet. Nothing touched you. You were free.

Isabel disembarked at Ostia Antica. The man went down the stairs ahead of her, and disappeared into the small crowd of people moving through the tunnel to the station's exit. By the time Isabel came out into the station hall, he had gone. The entire hall had emptied except for two women sitting beside each other on a bench. The younger one had her feet up on a big red duffel bag. Isabel went outside. The air was sharp after the warmth of the train, and she felt startled, as if she had just been woken up. A scooter flew by, and the pillion rider turned back and waved joyously at her before vanishing into the haze of orange streetlights.

"Perché mi sta sta sequendo?" said a voice behind her.

Isabel swung round. The man stood two feet from her with his hands in his pockets.

"Do you follow me?" he asked. He stepped forward and laid his hand on her scarf. His palm touched the top of her right breast. "From the Pantheon?"

Isabel said nothing. His hand still rested on her chest. Her heart surged up to meet it.

"Perhaps you want a drink?' he said. He looked at her steadily. "We can talk about it."

They went into a hotel a few blocks from the station. The

bar was empty, and the barman sat at one of the tables watching the small TV mounted to the wall. He stood and walked over to the bar, shooting the TV a longing glance. The man ordered them both a glass of wine. He led Isabel to the table furthest from the door. She took off her coat and scarf and laid them in her lap.

"You're visiting Italy? You're Inglese?" the man asked.

Isabel nodded. She played with the label on her coat. "Do you live here?" She didn't look at him.

"In Roma."

She glanced at his hand when he clasped his wine glass. He had thin sensitive fingers. "Are you an artist, photographer?" It was a stupid question, and she regretted asking it.

"No. Meccanico. Mechanic. Your first time in Roma?"

Isabel shook her head. "I came here in my teens. A long time ago."

"You like it?"

"It's beautiful. The pine trees and the colours of the buildings—ochre, terracotta. A dream."

He took a big sip of his wine. "You've seen the Fontana di Trevi?"

"Yes."

"You like that?" His tone was weighty as though the subject were of great importance.

"It's very beautiful."

He sat back satisfied. Isabel couldn't stand the Fontana di Trevi. She found it garish. She gulped back her drink and returned the glass to the table almost empty. He got up and ordered them another round. When he returned, he moved his coat from the chair opposite her to the chair beside her and sat down. Their thighs were touching.

"Why do you follow me?" he asked. "What do you want?"

Isabel leaned away from him so she could see his face better. "I don't know." She looked at her ruby-coloured wine in the low light of the bar. She swirled the glass. "It was an impulse."

"I think I know what you want."

Isabel stared at him. His tone was low and charged, and she felt tingly. He stood up and moved back to the other chair, but he left his jacket hanging beside her and her wrist rubbed against the cuff of its empty sleeve.

"Is this man with you at the Pantheon your boyfriend?" he asked. She nodded. He leaned back in the chair and crossed his legs. "You don't love him?"

Isabel didn't answer.

"You don't want to talk about this? What should we talk about? The European Union?"

"I do love him." Isabel took a sip. It was not the same wine as the first glass she'd drunk. The taste was rich and smoky. It reminded her of campfires.

"This is a strange love."

She looked down at her hands resting on the table. Her red nail polish was badly chipped. She picked at her thumbnail.

"Love is complicated," she said.

"Perhaps for you, but for me it's simple." His eyes were insistent.

Isabel half-smiled. She pushed her chair back and excused herself and went to the bathroom. In the mirror above the sink, she examined her stained lips and pink cheeks. Misgiving pinched her stomach. She exhaled and blotted her lips on the hand towel. When she came out, he was paying the bartender.

"Finish your drink," he said to her, pointing at her half-full glass on the table. She took a swig and put the glass beside his empty one. She gathered up her coat and scarf and waited for him by the door.

"Do you want to go upstairs?" he asked when he came over.

The man unlocked the door and switched on the light. The hotel room was sparsely furnished. There was a Michelangelo print screwed into the wall above the bed. Isabel stepped in to the room behind him, and he locked the door. He pulled her bag from her shoulder and tipped it on the floor.

"Hey!" Isabel bent down to try to scoop up the contents, but he shoved her away. She lowered herself on to the bed, dazed. "What the fuck are you doing?"

The man ignored her. He opened her wallet and took out the money. He turned her iPod over in his palm several times, and then he put that in his pocket too. Isabel got up unsteadily and tried to grab his arm. He shoved her back towards the bed. He tried the side doors of the television display cabinet. One was sealed, but the other revealed a mini-bar. He emptied the contents onto the carpet and separated out the three small bottles of vodka from the jumble of chocolate bars and crisp packets. Isabel stared at them.

He went into the bathroom, and she heard the shower curtain swish and the bathroom cabinet click and the sound of miniature shampoo bottles and moisturizers being knocked to the floor. She knew she should run away, but her thoughts were sluggish. They rose to the surface of her mind, thick as mud bubbles.

He came back into the room and placed a folding chair he found in the closet in front of her and sat so close that their knees almost touched. The space between them seemed to come alive. Isabel thought she could see the tiny movement of dust particles, as though millions of miniature jet streams streaked the air. Her head rolled back on her neck when she lifted it up to look him in the face. He was older than she thought—at least forty. He was unremarkable really. He began to speak to her in Italian, and then stopped. In the sudden silence, Isabel became aware of the buzz of the radio clock. It made her thirsty.

The man leaned towards her. He spoke at length now, jabbing the air with his forefinger for emphasis. Isabel lifted up her hands in a way that she hoped conveyed her commiseration.

"I don't understand. Please speak English."

He cut her off. His voice was loud, and this surprised her; she thought she was being so reasonable. A fleck of spit landed in her hair, and she flinched. At her movement, he reached over and grasped her firmly by both shoulders. She saw his hand holding her left arm, but she could not feel it, as if she had contracted from the surface of her skin. After a moment, he released her, and she sagged back into the support of the bed like something boneless. The man stood up and placed the folding chair back in the closet. He gathered up the vodka bottles and slipped them into his jacket pocket. He put the key to the room on the bedside table. Isabel heard the toilet flush in the room above. The water chimed in the pipes. The man unlatched the door and was gone.

Isabel sat on the bed for a long time, her body like a stone. Finally, she stood up and locked the door. She tried to tug the sheet and blanket back, but the housekeeper had tucked them in so fiercely that the effort was too much. She lay down on top of them, covering herself with her coat. The mattress was firm. It had no memory of anyone else's body.

Thin

Whale, baby hippo, disgusting blob. I imagine slicing the rolls of fat off my hips. I'll need a kitchen knife, a needle and thread. I can picture my body without its blubbery casing. I'm magazine thin. I'm gorgeous. I grab hold of my bulging stomach and pinch it between my fingers so hard I leave red lashes on my skin. *Chubby Chelsey.* No one actually called me that in high school. I started to get fat at fifteen, and teenage girls don't need alliteration to make you feel bad, they just look sideways at you in the mirror when you're at the sink washing your hands. Their eyes say *I'm so much better than you, fatty.*

I got the flyer for Dr Raymonds' Fat Dissolvers through my mail slot last Tuesday, printed on a folded A4 page of file paper. It looked as though it had been designed using Paint 3.1.

Next to a clip art picture of a stethoscope was the bold proclamation, in yellow and red Comic-Sans no less, that this patented compound of acai berry and ginseng and cassava root and agave would *work with my body's natural fat burning abilities to achieve never before seen results.* Dr Raymonds was excited to share his discoveries with me. He had only recently perfected his diet pill after a lifetime of scientific research. What's more, while Fat Dissolvers normally retailed at $49.99, as I would be one of Dr Raymonds' first customers, he wanted me to have the entire container at the introductory offer of $15.99. I mailed in the order form, and the package arrived yesterday.

I know the chances of Fat Dissolvers actually working are minute. I'm not stupid, but I've got to try. What's sixteen bucks compared to the chance of being thin? Besides, I'm pretty sure Einstein said that every great idea is scoffed at to begin with. Of course, every terrible idea is scoffed at to begin with too. Hope springs fucking eternal. I take three pills as directed and wash them back with coffee. I put the container in the top drawer of my desk.

I'm a cubicle girl for a big corporation downtown. Most people react with a mixture of distaste and pity when I tell them what I do, as if I've told them I have hemorrhoids. Sure, the work can be dull, but I like to challenge myself with the small stuff. For example, I don't think there's anything about Excel that I don't know. If there's a problem with a spreadsheet, no one calls Larry the IT Guy, they come and look for me.

Marissa, my cubicle mate and best friend, drops her oversized leather bag on the desk. She's fifteen minutes late. She undoes her coat and hangs it over the back of her chair. She's wearing a grey-striped wrap-over dress. She could be a model. The dress clings to her hips and lies taut across her flat belly. I'm wearing black pants and a black shirt. Not that the black helps; it just makes me look like a thundercloud. Cumulus Nimbus. The words even sound round. When I'm thin, I'll wear beautiful clothes. I'll lean into men and laugh. I'll stand at the end of a long pier and let the wind play in my hair. I'll buy a Labrador puppy and take him out jogging.

"Did you have fun last night?" Marissa sits down and turns on her monitor. "Paul from HR seemed nice. Did you get his number?"

"No." I bet Paul from HR wouldn't even remember my name, despite the fact that the three of us discussed ridiculous office policies for a few hours and he bought Marissa and I a beer.

"You could at least try." She looks at me disapprovingly. "You have to put yourself out there."

I make a face. I saw how Paul watched Marissa when she got up to go to the washroom. Men always look at Marissa that way. It's like she's the latest model of Ford truck.

"Did you see the memo about the Team Building Workshop for Saturday? Apparently we're going horse riding." Marissa rolls her eyes.

I hate corporate workshops. I'll do anything to avoid them. We went abseiling once; Marissa looked as though she was in a MEC photo shoot, I looked like a heifer hoisted up for slaughter. I try to avoid anything that involves moving my body while other people watch. I won't dance, I won't jog, and I definitely won't swim. I don't want anyone to see my cottage cheese thighs.

Marissa notices the fear on my face. "Don't worry, I'll think of a way to get you out of it," she says.

At 10 AM, I'm entering the monthly hydro usage into a spreadsheet, when I feel this sudden lightness, as if I'm floating in the ocean and I have been caught by the swell of a wave. I get up unsteadily and go into the washroom and splash some water on my face. In the mirror, I notice that my belly looks distinctly smaller. My black woolen pants feel looser. A thrill goes through me like a low-voltage electric shock. I'm scared to be hopeful, but I can't help it. This could really be it.

"I've lost weight," I tell Marissa while we're eating lunch in the cafeteria. "It's my new herbal diet pills."

Marissa takes a sip of water. Even after she's pulled the glass away, her lips stay pursed.

I pop the tab on my can of cola. "They speed up your metabolism. There's a guarantee. Thirty pounds in five days."

"I don't want you to be disappointed," she says. "Remember the magnetic power band?"

I don't say anything. I wore the magnetic power band around my head for six weeks. It was supposed to alter my brainwaves and suppress my appetite. All it did was stain my forehead navy blue.

"Besides," Marissa says. "Being fat doesn't matter."

That's what she's always telling me. She says that being obsessed with appearance is superficial, that no one cares about my weight except for me, that men are attracted to women for who they are, not what they look like, and the only reason I'm still single is because I believe I'm not attractive enough and that if I start believing I'm deserving of love no matter what I look like, someone will fall in love with my inner beauty. She took women's studies at university.

I nod. Last Christmas she bought me a book called *Dress for Your Shape*.

"You're the apple," she said and tapped her pink fingernail against a pencil drawing of a roly-poly pudding of a woman. "See how good she looks. There's no reason for you to cover up the way you do. You've just got to work it."

I flipped through the pages, and the apple-shaped woman went bobbing by, wearing loose-fitting tunics to hide her flabby tummy and diligently avoiding stripes and drawing attention to her ample bust with scoop necks. Oh, she was working it, all right, like a donkey dragging a cart of coal up a hill.

"You're perfect at any size," Marissa says. She's eating a Cobb salad with dressing on the side, and I'm eating chicken fingers. She points at my plate with her knife. "But the important thing is to be healthy, and that's high in saturated fats, you know. Even the littlest choices make a difference." She nods at me with encouragement.

Using the plate edge, I unhook the chicken finger from the tines of my fork.

After lunch, while most of the office is in yet another efficiency meeting, there's a paper jam in the Xerox machine. I go back to my desk and phone Larry for help. Larry's peering into the paper tray when I come up beside him.

He looks up at me and then jumps two feet to the right. "Jesus!"

"What?" I say, wondering if this is some kind of joke.

"Go look at yourself." He doesn't look like he's kidding. He looks scared. Do I have a chicken finger stuck between my teeth? I run to the washroom and look in the mirror. My face is angular. I must be like twenty pounds lighter. My clothes droop. I grab at the folds of my shirt. There really is nothing under there but air. I grip the edge of the sink. I'm transfixed. I can't believe it's finally happening.

By 4 PM, I look like the after photo in a diet advertisement; my pants are so baggy I could fit a second person in there. A mob of women from the third floor gather around my desk, and I stand sideways and hold my pants out with one hand and with the other I do jazz hands.

"This morning?" Lisa from Accounting says. "You started taking them this morning?" She turns the plastic pill container around in her hand, and the picture of Dr. Raymonds' bespectacled face and white lab coat disappear out of sight behind her palm.

"Yes." I have to hold my huge pants tight to my body. It's like I'm trying to wear a two-man tent. I've already been to the washroom and removed my underwear. They kept slipping down and snagging around my knees. I buried them in the paper towel disposal.

"What if you don't stop losing weight? You could just disappear." Cindy's a PA. Her bottom lip protrudes thoughtfully. "Where has all the, you know, *fat* gone?"

Lisa looks on the pill bottle for the answer. "Fat simply melts away," she reads. "That's all it says."

Cindy looks around the office discreetly as if she's expecting to see my melted fat pooled up under the air conditioning unit or flowing like lava towards the elevator.

I don't give a shit where it's gone. It could have evaporated. Good Riddance.

"The fat's been used up by my body. By my new fast metabolism." I grab the pill bottle back from Lisa. "I'm not going to disappear. The government tests this kind of stuff to make sure it's safe."

Cindy seems uncertain. "People lie," she says. "Haven't you seen *Erin Brokovich*?"

"Here." Marissa pushes through the crowd of women to place a pair of gym pants in my hands. "Come to the washroom."

In the washroom, I release my grip on the waistband of my pants, and they collapse around my ankles like a deflated parachute. The gym pants Marissa gave me are made of black Lycra with a purple waistband that folds over. They're the kind worn by skinny blonde girls who do yoga and like to drink wheatgrass and date singer/songwriters. I shimmy into them. I cannot stop staring at myself. I'm thin. I have hipbones that stick out. My stomach is concave.

"I think you should go and see a doctor," Marissa says. I look at her in the mirror. A little downward-facing arrow has formed above her nose.

"Mmmm." I turn sideways. My reflection turns too. I run my hands along the curve from my waist to my hips. I'm so beautiful. I should go to a candlelit bar wearing a black dress and sheer nylons and red high heels. I should go to the pool in a tiny bikini and ride the waterslide. I should go shopping.

"People don't lose weight like that. It's not right." Marissa stares too, but she doesn't look pleased. "It's dangerous."

"I doubt it. I feel amazing."

For a moment, we watch each other in the mirror. Marissa raises an eyebrow.

"I'll go to the walk-in clinic if it makes you feel better," I say. "But I'm sure everything's okay."

"Do you want me to come with you?" Her face is soft and full of concern.

"No. I'll be fine." My eyes slide back to my tiny waist and slender arms and the breathtaking curve of my pert breasts. I want to drink myself in.

I can see the clinic waiting room through the window. A kid with an impressively runny nose has built a complex fort structure out of magazines, and there's a man slumped over by the water cooler in what looks like deep despair. The receptionist gestures at me to come in. I hesitate. What if the doctor says something *is* wrong and reverses the process? I won't go back to being that repulsive blimp, a tub of lard, the jelly belly. I don't care about possible side effects; I'd rather be thin. I'm not giving this up before I've had a chance to enjoy it. I shake my head at the receptionist and walk away. On the corner, I take out my phone and call Marissa. She answers on the first ring.

"The doctor said these are very unusual results but that it's nothing to worry about," I say.

"Really?" She sounds doubtful.

"Yeah. Apparently my particular blood type has a tendency to be more responsive to metabolism triggers than other blood types." I pause to see if she'll buy this for even a moment.

"Did you tell him exactly how much weight you lost? Because it seems way more extreme than that to me."

I've missed my chance to cross the street. I press the walk signal again. "He said there's no doubt it's extreme, but it's still fine. It's a freak occurrence. Like that kid who jumped off the Golden Gate Bridge and lived and then was rescued by a seal." This all sounds pretty good to me. I'm beginning to suspect that I am the lucky beneficiary of a bizarre but benign fluke of chemistry or biology or something.

She doesn't say anything.

The traffic lights change, and I step out into the street. "I promise I'm fine, okay?"

"Okay. But you'll go home now and rest up? I'll come by after work tonight. I don't think you should be alone."

I don't go home. I go to Holt Renfrew, a store I've never been inside before. I'm pretty certain they employ an invisible force field to keep fat women out. But now I slip through the front doors and glide between the racks. I smile at the tiny sales girl with the flippy hair and sparkly eye makeup.

"Can you start up a change room for me?" I ask. She's the type of woman I would have normally avoided; with her svelte body, I'd have considered her rungs above me in the pecking order. If we had been a pair of stags, she'd have a huge set of antlers and be rounding up the herd for breeding and I would have been off hiding somewhere in the long grass. But now I'm willing to rub my antlers up against the nearest tree trunk. I want to scrape at the ground with a hoof and mark my territory.

In the change room, with the help of a black sequined mini dress, I discover I'm a size four. I want to kiss the label. I've imagined this moment so many times. I can't believe it's actually happened. Eight hours ago, a dress like this would have made me look like a misshapen sack of potatoes. I do a twirl and check out my ass in the mirror. It's perfect. Apricot-shaped.

"Could you bring me another one in blue, size four?" I tell the salesgirl when she raps on the stall door. I hope every woman in the vicinity hears me. I want an announcement in the paper. I want to clip the article and send it to my mother. I'll never be red-faced and sweaty with shame at the entrance of a fitting room again. No more inching past the salesgirl with a pair of size twenty pants doubled over my arm like the sheet set for a king-sized bed, hoping desperately that no one sees the label. I'll hold out my size four jeans like a passport. That's right, I'm one of you. I'm thin.

"Did you want to try anything else?" The girl says through the stall door. Her voice rises up at the end as though she's been squeezed.

"That's good for now." I lean back against the change room wall and admire myself. I can't stop staring at my clavicle, at the way it splays out, delicate and fine-boned as a pair of wings.

When I open my apartment door to Marissa, I'm wearing a pair of new grey sweatpants and a tight white tank top that clings to my flat belly. I feel like a starlet. When you're thin, you're glamorous in anything. A look of surprise crosses Marissa's face as if she'd been expecting good ole, lumpy Chelsey. She comes in, drops her purse on the carpet in the living room and sits down on the couch, where she smoothes her wrap dress down over her hips. I can see now there's a tiny roll of fat on her tummy that I never noticed before. I sit down beside her and tuck my legs up. There's no fat on me anywhere. I love how easily I fold. I love how small my body gets. I don't spill out of my clothes. I'm all angles. I can feel Marissa's eyes on me.

"I had to go shopping." I gesture at the clutch of shopping bags beside the couch. "Obviously."

Marissa frowns slightly. "I hope you didn't spend too much, or you made sure there's a good return policy, you know, in case the weight comes back."

I stand and stretch my arms out, and my tank top rolls up to expose my midriff.

Marissa stares at my stomach. There's an expression in her eyes that I can't quite read. Pain or maybe envy.

I tug my tank top down. "I'm not going to get fat again. I'll just keep taking the Fat Dissolvers."

Inside her bag, Marissa's phone beeps. "It's in the side pocket," she says.

I scoop her whole purse off the floor and pass it to her.

She pulls a face. "You could have just grabbed the phone." She reads her message. "It's Lisa. Everyone's going to Monty's at seven. She wants to know if we want to come."

"Yeah, why not?" I want to shine.

Marissa stands and nods her head in a considered way, as if she's beginning to understand something. "I'll go home and change first and meet you there then." She stops before she turns the handle of the front door. "You're sure want to come out?"

"You need to stop worrying." I reach past her and open the door. The smell of the hallway wafts in. Someone's cooking chili. "I'm totally fine."

Marissa slides by me. Her thighs brush against the door and jiggle a little.

"See ya," I say. I'm aware of the showiness in my voice. The little shrill of conceit.

I walk into Monty's wearing a sleeveless black dress with an asymmetrical hem. The girls are clustered around our normal table at the back. Cindy sees me first, and her mouth drops open like she has only just found out that Iraq and Iran aren't the same country.

Marissa looks up at me and then looks back at her beer. Then she moves to stand up. "Do you want a drink?"

"I'll get it." I saunter across the floor to the bar as if I'm part of an invisible conga line. I can feel people watching me, and I lap up their looks. I imagine every woman in the bar is comparing herself to me; I hope they feel cowed by the angles of my hips and humiliated by the effortless plane of my stomach. All those years spent sidling around hoping that no one would look at me, when I could have been living like this. Being thin is like winning First Prize. I order a dirty martini and tip the bartender two dollars.

"Thanks, sexy." He tosses a dishtowel into the sink.

"Watch your language," I say and wink before I sashay back to our table. I would never have had the guts to do that yesterday. Being thin gives you permission to take up more room in the world.

"Hey," Cindy says. "There's Paul from HR and Josh from Marketing." She waves them over.

Paul squishes into the booth beside me, and Josh slides in beside Marissa. Paul leans across and says hi to Marissa first, and then he turns to look at me.

"I don't think we've met. I'm...." For a moment, he looks kind of dumbfounded. He scrutinizes my face, and then he gets it. "Chelsey? Wow." He has to look away. "I heard about this at the office." He looks at me again and shakes his head. "Wow, I have to say you look incredible, Chelsey."

"Thanks." Hearing that could never get old.

"So, big day, then? You must be reeling."

"I am, but in a good way." I turn into him. My leg brushes against his suit pants, and my nylons crackle with the static we create.

Paul starts at the sound.

"How shocking!" I cover my mouth in mock horror.

"That's a terrible joke," he says, smiling. "Appalling." He stops and takes me in. "It's not just your looks that have changed. You were so cold yesterday."

"You weren't exactly warm yourself." I look over at Marissa. She's bent over her phone.

"Hmmm." Paul doesn't seem entirely convinced. "Would you like another drink?"

I nod and give him a flirty little jab on the forearm with my finger. "Make it a double."

I hated talking to men before; I felt like a bag of wet flour, I felt sorry for them, stuck talking to the fat girl. Now I feel like I'm fly-fishing, as though I'm nymphing for trout. I turn back to the rest of the table. Marissa is watching me with a funny look on her face. When she realizes that I've noticed, she lifts her glass in my direction but doesn't smile.

"Are you attending the team building thing tomorrow?" Marissa asks Paul when he brings my drink back. "Because I thought we could carpool?" She leans across the table in his direction and stretches out her arms until her hands almost touch his beer glass. She looks up into his face. Her hair falls suggestively into her eyes.

"Sure." He turns back to face me. "You should come too."

Marissa draws her hands back into her lap and straightens up. "Chelsey never goes to those things. She hates them."

"Actually, I was thinking about going." I let my arm brush up against Paul's, and the hairs on his arm tickle me.

"Good," he says, smiling.

Marissa leans back against the bench and takes a sip of her mojito. "You're seriously going to go horse riding?"

"Why not?" I run my finger around the base of my martini glass until it squeaks.

Marissa crosses her arms. "I'm shocked, that's all." She turns back to Paul. "So we'll carpool. I'll drive."

"Great, we'll try to make it fun, right?" He nudges me with his elbow.

"Sure will," I say.

Paul is already in the car when Marissa picks me up in the morning. He offers the front seat to me, but Marissa puts her hand on his arm before he unbuckles his seatbelt. I open the back door, admiring my reflection in the metallic blue paint of her Mazda before I get in. I'm wearing skinny jeans and a loose white peasant top. I blow-dried a slight wave in my hair. I want to swoon a little every time I catch a glimpse of myself.

Paul turns around in the seat. "Have you ridden a horse before?"

I shake my head.

Marissa twists around to glance at us.

"You'll be a natural, I'm sure." Paul smiles at me. It's a big gushy, radiant smile, and it sends a tingle through me.

Marissa makes a low noise at the back of her throat. "He's right. You'll do fine," she says tightly. "They'll probably just lead you round the ring." She looks at me in the rearview mirror. Her brown eyes are dark. Her voice softens, "I'll probably need to be led around too. It's been years since I've been on horse."

Cindy waves at us as we drive into the car park of the barn. She's leaning against the fence, wearing a pair of suede chaps over her jeans. Her ash blonde hair has been pulled into pigtails.

"Where do you even buy chaps?" I say under my breath as we get out of the car.

"You look so good, Chelsey," Cindy calls out to us. "I just can't get used to the thin you. I like your shirt."

The rest of the office has already arrived, except Lisa who's late because her babysitter stood her up and she had to drop off the kids at her mother-in-law's. Almost everyone looks unhappy. Mike from Payroll is glassy-eyed, and the collar of his shirt is half-tucked in. He smells like he's recently drunk six or seven cans of Lucky and then fallen asleep with his face in a basket of barbeque wings. He puts his elbow up on the fence and his head into his hand.

"We'll get started then," Todd, the human resources manager, says. He's wearing beige jodhpurs and a pair of leather riding boots. I think I've seen the entire outfit in Ralph Lauren's Fall Collection.

The instructor brings out a big chestnut horse. She jogs around the ring with the horse trotting along beside her. When she passes me, I can see the line of her panties through her black leggings. They dig into her butt so that, when she moves, she gets a funny bulge of fat above her thighs. She brings the horse to a standstill beside Todd.

"Who wants to go first?" Todd smacks the front of his own boot a few times with his riding crop and looks around at us.

I shrink back. I feel the familiar panic, don't pick me, don't pick me, I don't want to be seen, I want to disappear.

"Come on, it's easy, people," Todd says. The crop goes thwack, thwack against his boot. "The horse does all the work."

Marissa shifts from foot to foot. Paul looks at me. Mike from Payroll clears his throat, and it has a throat-clearing ripple effect. Even I give a half-hearted snuffle. But nobody volunteers. According to the group email Todd sent out, the point of this workshop is to create positive synergy. Given the lackluster vibe of this group, I'm not sure how Snowball the horse plans to accomplish that.

"Fine," Marissa says. "I'll do it." She overemphasizes the reluctance in her tone. "If no one else wants to." She steps out into the middle of the ring and strides towards the horse. Her tee-shirt is a tiny bit too tight, and it rides up into the small of her back. She tugs it down over her hips. "I rode quite a bit as a child," she tells the instructor. She makes a clucky noise and holds her hand out to Snowball, and he lowers his velvety muzzle into her palm and blows. She giggles, and then she looks around to make sure we're all watching her.

"Actually, I'll go first if you want." I hear myself say. I'm as surprised as Marissa. She lets her arm fall to her side, and Snowball jerks his head away from her.

"Sure." She lays her hand on Snowball's neck to calm him. "Sure," she says again.

I jam my foot in the stirrup and grasp the horn of the saddle the way the instructor showed me and try to hoist myself up, but nothing happens. It's as though my arms have turned to string. I feel this strange rushing in my chest. My vision begins to blur. I try to turn to look at the instructor for help, and my foot slides out of the stirrup. I'm doubled up beside the horse. I think I'm going to be sick. I can hear Marissa asking me over and over if I'm okay, but I can't straighten up. My stomach churns. I gag, and the vomit comes. It splatters on my skinny jeans and on the white-stockinged legs of the horse. Marissa gets me to sit down beside the mounting block and rest my head between my legs.

"I'll take you home." Marissa rubs my shoulders. "Can you stand up?"

The feeling of nausea has begun to subside. I get shakily to my feet. The entire office has collected in a clump in one corner of the ring, as far away from me as possible. Lindsay from Internal Auditing covers her mouth with her hand. Cindy and Paul are huddled beside the fence. They don't even look at me.

The motion of the car upsets my stomach. I sink down into the passenger's seat and close my eyes.

"Do you think maybe it's the pills making you sick?" Marissa says as we slow down for a traffic light. There's an undertone to her voice that makes me think she's not actually asking a question. I rub my brow with my fingertips. I can feel a headache starting around my eye sockets.

"Who knows? Maybe I'm allergic to horses." My temple hammers. It is starting to feel as though my right eyeball might implode. I press the bottom of my palm down into the ridge of my nose. The pressure is soothing.

"I think we should go to Emergency." Marissa accelerates, and my stomach lurches forward too. I groan. I'm not going to the doctor. This is going to pass. It's probably the combination of martinis and overexcitement.

"No," I say weakly. "Take me home."

When I get home, I go to bed, and I wake up in the early hours of the evening feeling better. There are several missed calls on my phone from Marissa and a text message from Paul saying everyone's meeting up for dinner at 7:30 PM and he hopes that I'm feeling well enough to come. It's already 7:45

PM, but I message Paul back and say I'll head to the restaurant. I don't even feel that embarrassed about puking up all over Snowball. It seems excusable, natural. Everyone pukes. It wasn't my fault. Compared to the scuba diving lesson where there wasn't a scuba suit big enough to fit me, this is a success.

Cindy, Lisa and Paul are eating chocolate mousse when I arrive. Marissa isn't having dessert. She's shredding up a paper napkin. She tears each piece smaller and smaller until her placemat is littered with napkin streamers.

"You made it." Paul pats the empty seat behind him, and I sit down. I cross my legs and catch him sneaking a look at my calves. Marissa's hair is all frizzy, wisps escape from her ponytail. They strike out towards the ceiling like miniature lightning bolts.

"You kinda missed dinner," she says. "And we're all pretty beat from the horse riding thing. I think we're heading home after this."

Outside of the restaurant, Marissa, Cindy and Lisa catch a cab together.

"There's lots of room for you," Marissa says to me as she climbs into the backseat.

"I'll wait for the next one. We're opposite sides of town anyway."

She looks at Paul and I standing side by side on the curb. We're almost touching, and I'm hyperaware of our proximity to each other, of his jean-clad legs, of the smell of his leather jacket.

"It's really not that much out of our way," she says.

"Besides you won't be able to go with Paul, either. He doesn't live near you."

"It's okay. I'll get the next one."

Paul shuts the cab door. Marissa's face is all screwed up. It's as if she's got a toothache. She makes the "call me" gesture through the glass.

"Well," he says as their cab pulls away. "Now that we're alone, how do you feel about sharing a ride home?"

Once we're inside the taxicab, Paul kisses me. His mouth is sweet and soft, like sucking on a jelly baby. He runs his hands over my breasts, grabs hold of my ass. As soon as we get inside his house, he starts to unzip my dress. I stop him.

"I have to go to the washroom," I say.

Inside the bathroom, I latch the door. The last time I had sex was three years ago, a drunken one-night stand closer in tone to mud wrestling than to lovemaking. I want this to go well. I redo my hair in the mirror and step back to look at myself. My dress is tighter. My stomach strains against the stretchy material, and two bulges have appeared above my hips. I've got a fucking muffin top. At first I stand there staring at myself in disbelief, then I tug my nylons up higher in case it's the elasticized waistband cutting across me in the wrong place, but it makes no difference. I've definitely got fatter.

I have to do something. I don't want Paul to see me this way. Am I going to balloon back up to my original size? Explode out of this mini dress like a sausage bursting out of its casing? This can't be happening to me. I tip the entire contents of my purse onto the floor. Nail polish bottles and tampons roll in all directions. I grab the container of Fat Dissolvers and shake three out into my hand. The tiny red gel caps collect in the centre of my palm. They look ominous in the yellow light. Maybe Marissa's right, and I'm putting my health at risk. The pills could be corroding my stomach lining or eating holes in my liver. Perhaps I'm seconds away from a crippling stroke, the blood surging wildly in my brain. I look at myself in the mirror again. I stare at the rolls of fat. Unsightly lumps. There's no way I'm going back to that. I tip my head and gulp back the Fat Dissolvers. Paul knocks on the door.

"Just a second." I turn both taps on. The water gushes into the sink. I'm not any thinner than I was five minutes ago. Why is this happening to me? I shake another Fat Dissolver out of the container. I know it only says to take three, but I want to make sure it works. Paul knocks on the door again. I put the pill in my mouth and swallow it.

"Okay, okay." I gather everything off the floor.

"I'm sorry, I have to go," I say, coming out of the bathroom. I hold my purse against my stomach.

"Is it something I did?" he asks.

"No, I'm..." Nothing comes to mind. I try again. "I'm...I just want to go home." I try to squeeze past him.

"I thought we were getting along." He seems genuinely upset. "Is there nothing I can do to convince you to stay? We can take it slow." He steps towards me, and I step back towards the wall. I'm terrified he's going to see my muffin top.

"Hey!" he says. "I'm not going to hurt you."

"I know. Really, it's not you. I don't feel well." I keep my back to the wall, and my purse firmly against my belly and inch towards the door. Paul sidesteps along with me in almost perfect time. We could be doing an odd version of the cha-cha-cha. Perhaps he'll try to dip me?

He opens the door for me. "Okay. Maybe we could try this again? I'll give you a call?"

"Sure." In order to keep my back to the wall, I have to slide around him, and so I end up standing facing him on his doorstep with my purse between us like a shield.

"Because I like you. You're smart and a lot of fun," he says.

I nod. I don't want to turn around because I'm afraid of how big my ass might be by now, so I stand there staring at him, and he stands there staring at me. We stand so long, the security spotlight goes out, and he has to wave vigorously for the motion sensor. I guess he thinks we're having a moment or something because, when the light comes back on, he leans against the door jam and tries to draw me into his chest. I stick my hands out and brace myself against his shoulders to prevent him from getting his arms around me and a tussle ensues. The tip of his boot scrapes my ankle. My elbow digs into his ribs. The strap of my purse bats up against both of our noses. When he lets go of me, we're both a little out of breath. He steps back, bewildered.

"I'm waiting for you to shut the door," I explain. He doesn't move. "Because I don't want you to watch me walk away."

"Uh, I think I can handle it," he says. "We've only just met. The heartbreak at this point is pretty minimal."

"Shut the goddamn door, Paul."

"Probably not going to call you," he says, closing the door in my face.

The entire bus ride home, I pat down my stomach and hips to check if the fat has shrunk. I want it to be gone. *Please disappear, please disappear*, I beg. When I get off at my stop, I look at my reflection in the glass of the bus shelter. The bulges over my hips look smaller, and I'm pretty sure my belly has slimmed down too. The pills are working; I'm going to stay thin. I walk the eight blocks home, and I check out my reflection in every store window I pass.

By the time I've climbed the stairs to my apartment, the dress is even a little loose on me. I can pull it over my head without undoing the zip. I stand in front of the mirror. There's no fat on me anywhere. My pelvis juts out. I'm gaunt as a greyhound. I'm so feather-light, I could be Kate Moss. I stare at myself, turning back and forth. I'm mesmerized by my own thinness. I cross the room and lie down on the bed. The duvet cover is cool and silky against my skin. I slide beneath it. The fabric strokes the tops of my breasts, and I roll on to my side and run my hands over the groove of my ribs, span my tiny waist. My fingers find the nub of each hip, the bones so sharp-edged, I catch my breath.

I wake up with a pillow partially covering my head. My phone is ringing. It's in the bed with me; I can feel it vibrating. I find it down by my left foot.

"Hello?" I say huskily.

It's Marissa. "Are you alone?" she asks.

"Yes." I put the pillow back over my face. It's too early for this.

"Good," she says. "I've made an appointment with Dr.

Raymonds himself."

"Jesus, Marissa, can't you let this go?"

"No. This is your health. It's important."

"Fine," I say, rolling over. "Give me the address, and I'll meet you there."

Dr. Raymonds' office is next to a kebab shop. He's placed a Fat Dissolvers sign in the bottom corner of the kebab shop's window. It's the same picture as on the pill bottle except there's a grease smear on the right-hand side of his face. The sign is taped up next to a photo of an immense chicken shish kebab.

"Target market, I guess," Marissa says, and she raps the glass over the word "Fat Dissolvers." From behind the counter, the cashier hollers something and wags his finger at us threateningly. Marissa ignores him. She presses the bell twice.

"Explain to me again why we're going to harass this man whose product *actually* worked for me?" I ask when the lock buzzes. Marissa nudges me hard in the small of my back. I open the door. There are Fat Dissolvers containers everywhere. They're perched on every available surface. They stand one on top of the other, so precariously balanced it looks as if they're cascading from the ceiling.

"Not exactly flying off the shelves, I see," Marissa says under her breath.

Dr. Raymonds is in the living room seated on a leather couch. He's wearing a maroon terry-cloth bathrobe, his bare legs crossed at the ankle. He has very shiny hairless shins, and I can't help but wonder if he polishes them. The giant cut-out of himself balanced against the back of the couch is more appropriately dressed in a lab coat.

"Which one of you has experienced the rapid weight loss?" Dr. Raymonds asks. His accent sounds vaguely Eastern European.

"Me," I say. My voice comes out all watery. I'm suddenly filled up with gratitude. I feel as if I'm a guest on *Oprah*. So this is the man that's made me thin. He's saved my life. He must be some kind of eccentric genius. "Thank you, thank you, thank you." I'm gushing like a beauty pageant contestant. I can feel Marissa looking at me in disgust, but I don't care. Who knew being thin made you so warm and fuzzy on the inside? I always thought all the pretty girls were just dumb.

Marissa interrupts. "We're concerned because Chelsey lost close to 60 pounds in about 8 hours, and we think this is incredibly risky." She sounds as though she's auditioning for a spot on *Law and Order*.

"Eight hours?" Dr. Raymonds' eyes momentarily lose their focus. He seems stunned by this information. "That's very fast, very fast indeed." He turns to look at me, cinching his robe tighter. "How do you feel?" he asks, but it doesn't seem as if he really want to know the answer.

"I feel great. Never better." I keep looking at Marissa.

"Well." Dr. Raymonds looks over at Marissa too. "I'd call this a success then."

"I wouldn't." Marissa's voice is cold and hard. "I'd call it reckless endangerment. You don't have any idea what is going on with Chelsey's body, do you? "

Dr. Raymonds' smile disappears. He puts his hands into the pockets of his bathrobe.

"This is all your fault." Her face is flushed, and the redness begins to move down her neck. "You need to find a way to reverse the process right now. Reverse it right now!"

"Hey! I don't want this reversed," I say. "I feel fine. I'm fine, right Dr. Raymonds?"

"Yes. If you feel fine, then you're probably fine." He's looking at a spot on the wall behind Marissa's head now. "There weren't a lot of long-term trials, but there's nothing to worry about; it's all natural ingredients, 100% natural. Thank you for coming by." In a show of surprising optimism, he stands up and holds his hand out to Marissa.

"You can't mess with people like this." Marissa's body quivers the way an Olympic sprinter's does moments before she bursts out of the blocks. Her arm launches out from the shoulder, and she points her finger right at Dr. Raymonds' forehead. "A real doctor is going to reverse this for Chelsey, and you'll be sued."

Dr. Raymonds stares up at Marissa as though he's a small boy who has been told off for stealing the sugar. I touch her on the shoulder, and she lets her arm drop to her side.

"I'm leaving," she says. "I'm leaving."

"Thank you, again." I move towards the door. Dr. Raymonds nods at me, dazed. He presses a container of Fat Dissolvers into my hands, and Marissa shoots him the sort of parting look I have only ever seen before on *Days of Our Lives*.

Once we're in the street, Marissa strides purposely towards the bus stop.

"You need to stop taking those pills. That man is not a

doctor. This is a total scam."

"How can it be a scam?" I walk briskly to keep up with her. "Look at me!"

"It makes no sense," Marissa says. "This must be so bad for your body."

"What is your problem?" I stop walking. Marissa stops too. "You should be happy for me, but instead you're determined to ruin this."

"I'm thin because I eat right and I exercise. Not because I take crazy pills," she says shrilly.

"So what? You could take Fat Dissolvers too."

"That's not the point." Her arms jerk with frustration.

"Then what?"

She doesn't answer.

"You know what I think? I think you miss having a dumpy sidekick who made you feel good about yourself."

"Yeah? What about you? Staring at yourself in every reflective surface, mincing about in your tiny dresses. You're not better than everyone simply because you're thin now."

"You don't know what it's like. Being fat is hell, it's like being a second-class citizen. I hated myself. I never felt good enough to go anywhere."

"It's all in your head," Marissa says. "You could have been this person before."

"If it's all in my head, then why does it make such a difference to *you* that I'm thin now?"

Neither of us moves. Marissa's mouth twitches at the edges.

"Okay," she says. "This is getting crazy, and I don't want

to say something I don't mean. I'll call you when we've both calmed down." She starts to walk away from me.

"So that's it?" I yell after her. She doesn't turn around. "Marissa!" She keeps walking. It's begun to drizzle, the drops tickle my face. I catch a glimpse of myself in the store window. My reflection wavers in the glass. There's hardly any excess to me. I fit the mould. I'm like the women on TV, the girls everybody likes. Why would I give this all up? I touch my stomach. There's a slight ridge of fat starting to form above the waistband of my jeans. The feel of my own blubbery flesh between my finger and my thumb makes me sick. I take the container of Fat Dissolvers out of my purse and shake a bunch into my hand and put them in my mouth. I don't even count them. Marissa's not right about this, she doesn't care about my health. She just wants to be the thinnest. I face the glass storefront and pull my shirt tight against my hips. The little roll of fat on my stomach is still visible. I can't stand it. I toss another Fat Dissolver into my mouth, tip my head back and swallow the pill.

One More Goodbye

The first time Ginny left Matt, she barely made it out the front door before she relented. She had the trunk of her car open and was putting her suitcase in, when he got down on his knees in the driveway.

"Please," he said, crying. "Please. I know it's me." She felt such a rush of tenderness for him that she got down on her knees too and took him in her arms. He pressed his head into the crook of her neck and clung to her. "I love you," he kept saying, as they held each other and rocked back and forth. "I love you."

I can help him, Ginny thought, I can fix this, I can save us.

"I love you too," she said.

Matt carried her suitcase back into the house. He laid it

on their bed as if it were made of glass. The duvet dimpled to receive it. He turned round and smiled at her, as though with this simple action he had set things right, as though there was nothing more to say. Ginny stood in the doorway, her arms loose at her sides. Inside her chest, a corkscrewing of doubt and dread. She put her hand up against the door frame and leaned in towards it. She bent at the elbow and then straightened her arm again, like a pretend push-up.

"So we'll try to do it differently," she said. Half question, half statement. She had sat in the library at one of the booths near the windows and flipped through books with titles like *Men Who Hurt The Ones They Love* and *The Invisible Pain*. It reassured her to see elements of her own life reproduced in text. "I think when you start to feel overwhelmed with anger, you need to breathe, and we have to talk to each other. We can practice. It doesn't have to be so crazy."

"Okay," Matt said and squeezed her round the waist, "Now let's stop talking about this." He nuzzled her neck, and Ginny shied away.

"Matt! I'm serious."

"Okay, it'll be different. I'll breathe." He leaned in and kissed her. Part of his lips pressed against the corner of her mouth, part grazed her cheek. "Let's go out for dinner," he said.

On Saturday night, Matt was in a good mood. Ginny balled up the wet dishtowel she held. "I've signed up for hot yoga," she said. "Twice a week. I can walk straight there from work and be home by 9 PM."

Matt was bent over tying up the garbage bag, his beer bottle held between his thighs. He stopped and set the bottle down next to the stove, let the bag droop, its mouth gaped.

"We have dinner together," he said. "How will that work?"

"How will what work?"

"How will we have dinner if you're at hot yoga?" he said it as if she were stupid, unkind, cruel.

"Matt, it's two nights a week." Ginny kept her voice low and soft. The same tone she might use to coax in a feral cat. "This means a lot to me. I really want to do it."

Matt drew the drawstrings of the garbage bag tight. The bag expanded like a puffer fish. "You break every arrangement."

"How can we arrange to have dinner together every night for the rest of our lives?"

"If eating with me means that little to you, then we'll just have dinner separately every night from now on."

"That's not what I'm saying." Her body turned towards him, supplicant and loving. *Please,* her body said. *Please see this my way. Please be reasonable. Please.*

"You can't have it both ways." Matt went out the kitchen door with the garbage. Ginny followed him.

"I'm gonna go out with Dustin tonight. Why would I want to watch a movie with you? You obviously aren't interested in hanging out with me." He opened the garbage container and chucked the bag in.

"Lots of people go to yoga," she said to his back. "It's normal."

Matt shut the lid. Ginny was standing so close behind him that when he turned around his face was only inches from hers.

"Do you mind getting out of my way?" He looked at Ginny as if she made him sick. As if the way she was behaving was so obnoxious, he couldn't bear to be around her. Ginny stepped aside, and Matt went back into the house. He latched the door behind him, locking her out. Turbulence. Ground rupture. Quicksand. Ginny grabbed the door handle and pulled. The door didn't budge. Why was he so angry? She couldn't create the distance to look at this properly. There was no space inside her. She knocked on the windowpane and called his name. She wanted to make this better. She wanted to undo it. She couldn't stand to feel as if she was hated, as if she was abandoned. She would do anything to make it stop. Matt opened the door.

"Please," Ginny said. "I don't want you be unhappy."

He didn't answer, but he stepped back and let her inside. They stood in the entrance way looking at each other. Ginny waited for him to say something, to apologize, to explain. Everything was tolerable if they were on the same page, if he was trying.

"Did you want to make popcorn? I'll get the DVD set up," Matt said, and he disappeared into the living room. Ginny went into the bathroom and locked the door. She let the cold tap run.

"He's a cunt," she said to the mirror. "He's a fucking monster."

Matt knocked on the door. "It's all ready to go, Gin-Gin," he said.

"I'll be right out." She splashed her face, and then she leaned into the mirror and looked herself in the eye.

The second time Ginny tried to break up with Matt, she made it as far as her sister Margot's with nothing but her purse and the bag of groceries in the back seat of her car. She started crying as soon as she stepped through the door, all of her sadness unloosed, and Margot held on to her shoulders and said, "What is it? What is it?" into her hair.

Ginny didn't know where to begin. She couldn't hold on to the thread of her story anymore. Matt's version always superseded hers. Two was a dangerous number. If there were just two of you, who got to decide who was right and who was wrong? There were gaps. Disruptions. He acted as though nothing had happened. He told Ginny she was overreacting. She kept a list because she thought if she committed everything to paper she could stop this shifting of her reality.

The time I snuck out of bed to finish folding the laundry and watch a movie and he woke up and I wasn't in the bed and he threw the laundry everywhere and ripped the power cord out of the wall. The time he insisted I share my email password with him because he said having a private email account was the same as keeping secrets. The time he followed me to Leah's house, to make sure I wasn't lying about where I was going. The time he instigated a twenty dollar fine system for when I didn't return his calls within half an hour.

But how could she show this to Margot? This list of crimes. Her own bad date sheet. Surely Margot would think that Ginny deserved it. After all, she kept standing on the same street corner, she kept getting into the car.

Ginny put her hands up to her face, and Margot let go of her.

"Tell me what's going on, Gin," she said. "You're scaring me."

Ginny opened her mouth to say something innocuous like, "Just a bad day at work," or "I'm about to get my period," but the truth came pouring out. A strange and garbled litany that Margot recoiled from, turning her body sideways against the wall as though she could not bear to hear this face on. Was it shock or disbelief? Ginny didn't know.

"This isn't your fault," Margot said finally, but Ginny felt as if a veil separated them and the words wouldn't connect. Margot reached out and took her elbow. "We'll sort this out." She guided Ginny to a chair, and Ginny sank into its softness.

"Break it off any way you can. You need to get out of this. You don't have to tell him in person. I can help you." Margot brought her carrot sticks with hummus.

Even as a kid, Margot had tried to soothe Ginny with food; saving her the red jelly babies, passing the roast potatoes off her plate when Aunt Yolanda had her back turned. At their parents' funeral, Margot had collected plateful after plateful of cocktail sausages and squares of cheddar on the end of toothpicks and miniature vol-au-vents and florets of broccoli to bring upstairs when Ginny refused to go down to the reception.

Their parents died in a car accident when Ginny was ten. A drunk driver overtaking on a blind rise. Both cars ended up in the ditch. The front end of their parents' Saab concertinaed in like an accordion. Their mother died on impact. Their dad was in a coma for a few weeks, but then he died too. Margot and Ginny moved into Aunt Yolanda's one-bedroom apartment.

"We'll just have to make do," Aunt Yolanda said. "I never planned to have children."

Ginny thought this was wise of her. It wasn't that Aunt Yolanda adapted to motherhood terribly, it was that she didn't adapt at all. Margot and Ginny slept on the pull-out couch in the living room for three years before they moved to a bigger house. Every morning, Ginny made Margot shift the coffee table back in from the hallway and place the money plant back on its yellowed doily before Aunt Yolanda woke up, as if by making themselves as unobtrusive as possible, she would love them more. But it only made it easier for her to forget they were there.

At Margot's kitchen table, everything seemed possible. Ginny felt as though she had returned from a war zone, as though she'd been turned up to high for days and days and now she could safely come back down. She blew her nose.

"You don't even have to go home again." Margot got a bottle of San Pellegrino out of the fridge. "I can collect your stuff for you."

Ginny went along with it all; agreeing to call Matt at 5 PM as soon as he was done work, accepting the pen and paper Margot passed to her so she could write down the list of essential things Margot would go and collect for her. But while she washed her hands in the bathroom, she knew she wouldn't do it. It was fine to talk about this, but it wasn't as easy as Margot made out. Telling Matt felt like an insurmountable task. A betrayal. She was tied to Matt, their lives enmeshed. She couldn't simply cut herself out of this. She wasn't that kind of animal. There must be another way. She pressed the backs of her hands into the grey towel hanging beside the sink.

Margot was making spaghetti and meatballs. She wore an apron with a picture of Snoopy on it. A bit of tomato sauce splattered across the bib and dribbled down the side of Snoopy's snout, making him look as if he had a head wound. Ginny stood against the fridge.

"It's better if I go and talk to him by myself. I'll call you, I promise." She leaned over and kissed Margot on the cheek. Margot held up the spatula as though it were a conductor's baton, but before she could speak, Ginny slipped out the door and went back to him.

After that, Ginny wished she'd never brought up her relationship with Matt to Margot at all. It complicated things. Some part of her felt that if she had never told anyone it wouldn't be true; as though Margot's knowing gave what was happening a name, gave it weight, made it real.

"He's different now," she told Margot when she met her for breakfast a week later. "He understands."

Margot nodded, but her face was disbelieving. Ginny signalled to the waitress for a coffee refill.

"He doesn't do it out of malice, he does it because he's scared," she said.

Margot prodded her egg, and its pale yellow yoke washed over the edge of her toast. She stared at it for a moment, and then she looked back up at Ginny.

"I'm not going to go on about this, and I know you love him, but it's only a matter of time before he starts hitting you. This is textbook cycle of violence stuff. "

Love him? Ginny said nothing. Love was not to be trusted. Love couldn't be used to make decisions. Love didn't tell the truth about other people. Love was just a feeling. It didn't mean anything. She thought about lying on the backseat of Matt's car with one foot braced against the backdoor and the other foot against the headrest of the driver's seat. She had watched as his mouth travelled down to the waistband of her jeans. His hands skimmed under her shirt, and where his fingers touched her, her skin radiated ripples of goose bumps. Was that what happened to everyone? That feeling of warmth and wonder, like being hot-buttered? He paused and looked up into her eyes. He was breathing heavily, his face flushed. The rings around his irises were darker. Ginny's heart dilated. She'd never loved anyone more.

"Will you marry me?" he said.

And she'd not even hesitated. "Yes," she said, and his mouth was on hers. In that moment, she *knew* they were meant to be together. She had never had such a sense of rightness, of certainty.

The waitress brought the coffee. Ginny punctured the lid of the creamer with her fork.

"It's all going to be fine," she told Margot. It didn't feel fine.

The third time Ginny tried to leave Matt was when she wouldn't go to Whistler for the weekend on a ski trip with Kelly and Adam.

"But I've already told them you're coming," he said on Friday morning when Ginny refused to get out of bed.

"I don't care." Ginny bundled the duvet around her shoulders and sunk lower into the bed. "I said I wasn't interested in going when you asked me the first time; why would you tell them that I was?"

Matt avoided the question. He tried to yank the duvet off of her. Ginny gripped her end. He pulled harder. Every time she drew a line, he crossed it.

"Get up," he said. She turned her face away from him, clasping the duvet so tightly her knuckles whitened. He jerked forcefully, and the duvet tore out of her hands, hurting her. She made a plaintive noise. She had to dramatize her pain because he always ignored it. She tucked her knees up to her chest.

"Get up."

"I'm not going. Go by yourself."

"Don't be stupid. It's a couples' ski trip. It won't be a couples' ski trip if you don't come."

Ginny didn't move. Matt left the room and came back with a glass of water. He poured it on her. The water soaked through her pyjamas. It pooled around her knees and started to soak through the sheet and into the mattress. Ginny lay still. She knew from experience that Matt never really backed down; every time she stood up to him, his behaviour escalated. He one-upped her. She lay in the cold wet bed pretending nothing had happened. If she could show him that she chose how to respond, he would understand he couldn't control her. Matt went and refilled the glass of water. This time he poured it over her head. Ginny screamed. She threw the pillow at him but missed and hit the dresser instead. The pillow landed near

Matt's feet. It left a wet spot on the dresser's yellow painted doors.

"You're torturing me." She got out of the bed. "This is abuse. You're abusing me." She looked at him. She wanted him to acknowledge what was happening, but he wouldn't. His eyes blanked hers.

"I can't do this anymore." Ginny went into the bathroom and locked the door.

"Me neither," Matt said through the wooden panelling. "If I go on this ski trip by myself, I won't be coming home."

"Good," Ginny said. She held onto the door handle and trembled. She wanted him to leave her. It would be so much easier if he did the work of breaking up, if he cut her off. She peeled off her wet pyjamas and got in the shower. The water streamed through her hair. There's something wrong with me, she thought, why can't I just walk away from him? I'm like a dog with its own vomit. The shampoo got into her eyes. Her right eye smarted, and she pulled the eyelid down and tried to rinse it out. She realized she wanted something contradictory. She wanted Matt to leave, but she didn't want to feel it. She wanted an exit that caused no suffering.

When she came out of the bathroom, Matt was sitting on the bed.

"I called and cancelled." He cradled the phone in both of his palms so gently it could have been a tiny animal. Ginny picked up the wet pillow and laid it back on the bed. She couldn't bear to go through everything all over again. She was so tired.

"Okay," she said. Okay. Okay. Okay. Okay. Okay.

"What do you see in him?" Margot asked her, as if Matt were in possession of some secret attribute that counteracted all of his other behaviour in Ginny's eyes. An antidote.

Ginny didn't answer. They were in the supermarket.

"Look," she said. "The okra's on sale." And she unwound a plastic bag from the roll beside the oranges and gave it to Margot.

Ginny hadn't seen Matt at all. That was the problem. That had been the problem all along. They'd met at a barbeque hosted by a mutual friend. Matt kept his eyes on her while he turned the steaks. He smiled at Ginny as though he knew something about her other people didn't know. It made her feel shy. At the drinks table, she had fumbled with the plastic cups. She liked how he looked. The slimness of his body and how he moved. He was solid and graceful at the same time. His jeans were a little ratty at the bottom. There was something about his physical presence that made her feel as though she were soft-centered, gooey in the middle. Ginny had never been in love before, and she yearned to be, more than anything. In university, she'd dated but never the boys she liked. She stayed away from the ones who made her feel as though she had stood up too fast. If they met her in the hallways with a coffee in hand, she couldn't talk to them. Her voice, high-pitched and the words rushing out of her. She felt as if she had no armour on. She escaped by ducking into the ladies' washroom or pretending she had somewhere else to be.

When Matt asked her to hold the tongs while he went to get the corn on the cob, she had thought she was choosing something different. She'd let his fingers brush against hers. She'd looked into his eyes.

"I know he can be really charming." Margot twirled the bag of okra and tied a knot. "It's easy to fall for that."

Ginny put the bag in the cart. She nodded. Sometimes she told herself that Matt had not been this way when they met, as though she were living a fairytale in reverse and her prince had morphed into a beast, but she knew she'd wanted love so badly she had chosen to believe things that weren't true.

They held their wedding reception in the banquet hall at the Ramada. The hall was perfect: spare and elegant, tea lights floated in votive cups; dried fern, latifolia and hydrangeas were arranged in giant copper vases. Her dress cost two thousand dollars. The satin brushed against her skin like lips.

You're so beautiful, everyone kept on saying. *Matt's the perfect husband. He comes from such a good family.*

Everything in her life had finally added up right. She felt hard and cold. Shiny object, desired and admired, held up to the light. A precious stone. Nothing hurt her. Were her bridesmaids full of envy? Jealous of her good-looking husband? Heady with her own success, she hoped so.

When the dancing started, she went to find the bathroom but ended up downstairs in some sort of service area with no windows. It was nice in the dark, out of sight of everyone for a moment. She leaned into the smooth concrete wall and pressed her palms against its coolness.

Once Matt had redecorated their living room without telling Ginny. She'd been out for the day helping Margot move into a new apartment. When she arrived home, Matt met her in the driveway, excited. He could barely wait for her to get out of the car. He grabbed her purse from her and took her hand and led her into the house. Two giant russet-brown leather sofas jostled around a metal and glass coffee table, everything so dark and austere.

"What do you think?" He rested his hand on the back of one of the sofas in the manner of a confident salesman.

Ginny had intended to redecorate for ages. She'd pictured blues and greys, the colours reminiscent of a beach house. "It looks nice," she said without feeling.

Matt's body stiffened. "You don't seem sure."

"I like it."

He crossed his arms. His knees locked. His stance reminded Ginny of the Fat Controller in *Thomas the Tank Engine*.

"What do you like best then?" There was an edge to his voice.

Ginny looked back and forth between the table and the sofas. She couldn't stand any of it. "I like the glass in the coffee table."

Matt threw his hands up. "If you didn't lie to me all the time, I would trust you more."

Ginny hesitated. "I don't like it," she said.

"What the fuck? I don't even know why I bother with you. I spent the whole day doing this. You're so ungrateful."

"I'm not ungrateful." She looked up at him. "I just really don't like it."

"Whatever. You can take this all back to the store tomorrow by yourself." He stomped out of the room.

"Matt," she called after him. "We can make this work. We could get cream curtains or something."

He didn't answer. She touched the sofa. The leather was cold and uninviting.

"If you didn't yell at me every time, maybe I'd tell you the truth more," she said to the empty room.

Ginny went into the kitchen and made dinner, frozen lasagna and a big salad. She laid the table. She placed the fruit bowl in the middle as a centerpiece. One of the bananas had brown spots. If she appeased him, eventually he would understand she didn't mean to hurt him, that she wasn't dangerous. She was the dog in the fight that rolled over and showed its white fluffy throat.

"This is nice." Matt said when he came in for dinner. "How was the move? I'll bet Margot wasn't even half packed when you got there." He reached over and rubbed her hand. She resisted pulling back. She couldn't erase his behaviour the way he could. He acted as though he lived in a world that was all foreground, where he focused only on the view closest to him.

"Margot was completely packed, actually." Ginny withdrew her hand and picked up the knife. She cut into the lasagna. The layers came loose.

Ginny counted the time she tried to talk to her mother-in-law about Matt as her fourth escape attempt, though it was closer to a kamikaze mission than a breakup. They were over for Sunday lunch, and Ginny had just finished serving trifle into dessert glasses while her mother-in-law cling-wrapped leftover pork chops. Ginny licked the spoon and stuck it in the dishwasher. A half-formed idea flitted through her mind, perhaps his family could take responsibility for Matt, take him off her hands, somehow.

"Matt tries to control me," she said. Now that she had spoken aloud, the concept seemed nebulous, impossible to explain.

Her mother-in-law snagged the piece of cling-wrap she was unwinding and tore off a jagged strip. She put that piece on the counter.

"He gets angry when I go places without him, he spies on me. He goes through my email. Sometimes I think he listens to my phone calls." She wished to stuff the words back inside of her, but they kept coming. "I don't think I can take any more. I'm telling you because I think he needs help."

Her mother-in-law's hands stopped moving. "Professional help?" she asked. Her voice was soft, and Ginny could see her face reflected in the kitchen window. Her eyes looked dewy, liquid brown like a deer's. Ginny moved closer. She hugged the edge of the counter as if she were walking a precipice.

"Maybe you could suggest to him that he see a counsellor? I've read some stuff, and I think maybe Matt has Narcisstic Personality Disorder or something like it. Obviously I don't know, but I don't think the way he acts is normal."

Her mother-in-law turned around. Over flushed cheeks, she looked at Ginny as if she had suggested that Matt was half-crocodilian. She tugged the cling-wrap tight under the plate of pork chops and passed it to Ginny.

"That sounds a little overblown. I'm sure if you talk to him again, you'll be able to work it out. I'll help you carry in the trifle, shall I?"

Ginny's bowl of trifle sat untouched on the dining room table in front of her. She dissolved a sugar cube into her coffee.

"Got a sweet tooth today?" Matt asked laughing. "You don't ever have sugar in your coffee." He ran his fingers down the length of her forearm. "You're always off in the clouds."

Ginny looked up and smiled, and the silver teaspoon in her hand went on stirring—clink, clink, clink against the bone china mug.

On her fifth breakup attempt, Ginny checked into a Travelodge in Abbotsford for the weekend without telling Matt where she had gone. The room was poorly cleaned, and through the window that wouldn't open, thin winter light fell in patches. Ginny lay on the bed. The pressed sheets held the faint odour of cigarettes. Being alone was insufferable. She felt unmoored, in withdrawal. This isn't real, Ginny told herself. She only had to make it through these first few days, and this wild feeling, this mixture of fear and loneliness, would abate. Think about it as swimming across a river, she told herself; you only have to make it through this dark water. You only have to make it through this. That was the worst part, the knowing better. She knew their relationship was poison, but she wouldn't stop. Zombie. Sleepwalker. She shut her eyes.

Ground yourself, Margot always said. Ginny tried to picture a field, somewhere without asphalt. Dirt.

The next morning Ginny went to Wal-Mart. She wanted to be somewhere safe. She bought socks and a new pair of tights. The checkout girl was young, her face lightly freckled, soft and open. She had a streak of purple in her mousy hair.

"$15.40," she said, holding the bag out to Ginny, who clutched it to her chest. "Do you want your receipt?"

Ginny shook her head. She wanted to be her, to be at the beginning of everything all over again. I can't reach you, she wanted to say. I'm living under glass.

In the car park, she sat in the driver's seat with the bag in her lap. It began to rain, the drops pocking against the windscreen. Where else could she go? Clouds, low and misty, pooled against the edge of the visible world. Air behaving like water. The horizon disappeared. Everything that held her in place had been yanked away at the same time. She switched on her phone and dialled Matt's number.

"Are you coming home?" he asked.

Ginny rested her forehead on the steering wheel. The hard plastic dug into her skin. Her decision wasn't rational. She didn't make a tally of Matt's pros and cons. He didn't have to persuade her. It wasn't sexual magnetism. It wasn't even optimism. She just didn't know how to be out in the dark water alone. She turned and swam back towards the shore.

Matt opened the door to her. She stood on the step.

"It's going to be different." He took her in his arms. Ginny let him hold her, but his words held no sway over her. This whole act was a force of habit that gave her nothing. It made her sick. You're a fucking junkie, she said to herself. You've built up such tolerance that even shooting the whole bag straight into your veins brings no relief.

He kissed her. Her lips kissed him back.

Matt was at work. Usually, Ginny liked having the house to herself, but now even when she was alone she felt as if she were under a shadow. A shade dweller, always in the cool of the rock. She sat on the couch with her feet on the table and drank coffee and ate a piece of cherry pie off her chest without using a plate. On TV, the talk-show host in her low-cut peach dress asked the battered wife in her badly fitting jeans and oversized smock top, "Why don't you leave him, Maureen?"

Maureen looked thoughtful, then she said, "I keep thinking it's going to be different. That he's going to stop any day now. And I love him."

The studio audience clucked and booed and hissed like barnyard animals. *Oh, he ain't ever going to change, honey.*

Ginny put her mug down. Maureen wasn't stupid. Tell them the truth, Maureen, tell them as a child you couldn't bear to pour hot water on ants, tell them you never thought another human being would like you, tell them you can't stand him. Tell him.

When Ginny finally left Matt for good, there wasn't much to take. A small suitcase. Her jewellery box. She wondered why she had spent so much time agonizing about how to divide their shared stuff. Lying in bed awake for hours, with Matt asleep beside her, she had felt the weight of the Bosch front-loading washing machine, the leaf blower, the Kitchen

Aid mixer. In some ways, she had used these things to keep herself tethered, to hold her in this particular orbit. They meant nothing to her now. She locked the door behind her and put her key back through the letter box. She heard it skitter across the pine floor.

For a while, she sat in her Nissan in the driveway with the engine running. Two semicircles appeared as the windshield defogged. She had read somewhere that eventually even the moon will leave the Earth. It's moving away at two centimetres a year. Miniscule shifts until suddenly it's gone.

Into the Blue

You could be watching from a position outside the frame. The rain has stopped. Steam rises from the tarmac. The pines drip. A 1993 blue Ford truck towing a camper comes round the bend. In the fullness of the corner, the front left tire on the Ford blows. The force of the implosion drags the truck left across the central divide so fast it defies logic. The Ford connects hard with a white Golf travelling in the opposite direction. At impact, it is as though both cars sit motionless, stuck, and then they pirouette away from each other, sending out a spray of glass and metal. You don't hear anything. The volume's turned right down. The Ford lands upside down in the ditch. The front wheels keep on spinning after the rear wheels have stopped. The camper is still on the road, lying on its side like a felled horse. The Golf crumples into a tree. The volume comes back up. The distorted metal shudders and tries to return to its original shape, to undo what has happened. Shards of glass drop from the shattered windscreen, little pings against the tarmac. A spaniel climbs out of the empty back window of the camper. He stands in the middle of the road, his tail between his legs.

It didn't hurt. Blood came out of your mouth. Red and rich, sticky as ore. Your arms were pinned against the seat by something that shouldn't have been there.

"Are you okay?"

The question came from behind, and you tried to turn to your head. Someone somewhere was crying. You could see the last of the mist burning off the pines. The sun trying to push through the clouds.

"We're going to get you out."

You wanted to nod, but you couldn't remember how. The Jaws of Life cutter tore into the roof. The lights of the ambulance turned the trees red, blue, red, blue. You lay on the stretcher and smelled chlorinated pools and the car park of the fast-food restaurant you worked in as a teenager. The air full of chemicals and grease. Sirens squealed into life as though they had only now been alerted to the urgency.

The ambulance drives away. A man sprays sand over the oil spill and sweeps the debris to the side of the road. Glass lies in the ditch and sparkles, a sudden seam of diamonds. It grows dark, and the tow truck comes. Men in orange safety vests truss up the camper. They hook the Golf to the tow truck, bumper first, and it rises out of the ditch. The tow truck drives away, the Golf swinging uselessly behind it like an arm in a sling.

You are alone now. Somewhere above and behind you, the wind moves through the pines. You want to sit up, but you have no sense of your own body, you're simply consciousness. It's like being on Ketamine. You are just in things. Right now you are in the asphalt. You can feel it cooling, the slight variations in temperature down through the bitumen to the sand and gravel base.

"I've been in an accident," you say to yourself. "I'm in shock. This is going to pass."

Water seeps into alligator cracks on the hard shoulder. You sense the crystalline bonds forming as water turns to ice and expands against the edges of the cracks. It reminds you of an allergic reaction, your tongue too big for your mouth. You vibrate with the rumble of tires. Stop, you want to say to the BMW as it rolls over you. The blonde girl driving is singing to Aimee Mann. You catch the chorus of *Wise Up*, and you can almost smell the car interior, cherry lip balm and body odour, but mostly you feel how the tires wear off the sharp edges of aggregates in the asphalt, stripping the bitumous film.

It must be late, after midnight; you'd left Penticton at 6 PM, and it's been hours since then. There's hardly any traffic on the highway now, but you can still sense the road unfurling. You feel the push and pull of it. You listen to the pines moving. You want to take deep meditative breaths, but you have nothing to breathe with. You must be hallucinating, probably on a high dosage of morphine. You're in the Fraser Canyon hospital in Hope, or perhaps you have been airlifted to Vancouver. Saul has been notified. He's beside your bed, or he has just gone out into the hallway to get coffee. You will open your eyes, and he will say, "You scared everyone stupid."

He will say, "You're fine, you big baby."

He will say, "This means the ICBC premiums have quadrupled, and you owe me one white Golf, but I'll accept a donkey in lieu if you've got one."

You try to picture Saul's face, visualize it in so much detail that it becomes real. His pale skin, translucent as a gecko, his hair and thin beard, the colour of custard. You don't love him, not in the cosmic way that romantic comedies say you should. Instead, you've made do with each other. He suggested once that you should probably get divorced, but you never got round to it. It's the worst kind of bad relationship because it's functional. You're as used to each other as you are to the pink pinstriped wallpaper in the living room that you've been meaning to strip off for years. You've both faded into the background. Funny then that you should think of no one else but him now.

You remember how once, angry and a little drunk on a beach in Mexico, you told him the art gallery meant more to you than he did. You never took that back. You just went to breakfast the next morning in your sunglasses and pretended it never happened. Besides, at the time you meant it.

But if you're thinking about only him now, perhaps it is love. Maybe that's what love is. He's solid, predictable, normal, and right now all you want is to go back to normal. But he never made the hairs on your arms stand up. Maybe thinking of Saul isn't working precisely because you don't love him, so you think of Zulu instead. Zulu who climbs into bed with you, puts his wet nose on your cheek, whose warm body presses against you. Please, open your eyes.

You must be in a coma. You always thought a coma would be gentler. You imagined a whiteout, a spa visit for your brain. No thinking, just sensing without judgment, the same state your yoga instructor exhorts you to get into during savasana. The sun rises, and on the hard shoulder, the ice melts in the alligator cracks; it tickles. An overloaded eighteen-wheeler grinds the tarmac and displaces the gravel base so that the surface of the road bows a little under the tires. You feel a rut beginning like a twinge in the knee or ankle.

You try to do what you've always done. Make the best of it. Take the long view. Get interested, take mental notes, and when you wake up, you'll write a best seller and end up on CBC with Shelagh Rogers.

You seem to be moving away from the road. Instead of feeling the buzz of tires on the grey Honda sedan, you compress and rarefy, crest the wave of sound as the car passes you by.

Maybe you're dying. This stops you. For a few moments, you just are, and you're indistinguishable from the air. You rise up with the heat coming off the asphalt, and you expand as you drift towards the pines, cool air below nudging you along.

Why did this happen to you? You remember being twenty-five and lying in your roommate Cassie's arms, crying over yet another breakup.

"Oh, honey, you're going to meet the right man." Cassie tucked her long brown hair behind her ears, and her silver bracelets ran backwards down her arm, tinkling. "Everything happens for a reason."

The thought that some divine power engineered events in your favour comforted you. Years later when Saul was laid off in the dot-com bust and he sat at the kitchen table wearing yesterday's clothes, staring morosely out the window, you told him, "Things will work out, everything happens for a reason."

He turned and gave you a withering look. "You're conflating reason with purpose. Every event is not leading up to some inevitable positive goal. Things happen because of your past actions and the laws of nature. I wasn't laid off so in the future I can get my dream job. I was laid off because the company's stock was overvalued."

"How can you live in a world like that?" you asked. "There's no sense to anything."

"There's no purpose, but the world still makes sense, it's just that nothing's in our control."

"I refuse to believe that." You opened the fridge. "Do you want pork chops for dinner?"

Saul just stared at you.

There's only a purpose, you realize now, if something happens after. If this is the end, then everything is meaningless to you. You are dying because of a Ford front tire. For something as simple as the incorrect pressure. Too soft, and so the sidewall flexed and split. Or perhaps that morning, the driver hit a curb when he stopped to get gas, and the layers of tire separated and air got between them and a bubble formed. You want to blame someone. You blame the Ford driver for his carelessness, for not carrying out thorough vehicle maintenance. You hope he's dying too. You've never checked the tire pressure on the Golf, but that's not the point; you didn't know. You would now. There should be more car maintenance awareness. Ad campaigns.

You cool, drift down again towards the earth. At the base of a pine tree, you crinkle through fallen leaves and twigs and sink into the humus, comforted by the soil, cradled by its warmth. You hear the low gurgle of a burrowing earthworm. You remember your grandfather in his garden holding out a handful of dirt and saying, "A good farmer is always a worm farmer." Without worms, there would be no soil; without soil, there are no crops; without crops—everything connected.

Were you so precariously balanced that this could have happened to you at any moment? Was life always like this? The thought startles you. You have not lived that way. Dying happened to other people. You think of those evenings in university, up late in the communal kitchen in the dorms, discussing what you would do if you learned you had only a year to live. Give up school, go to Peru, do acid, spend your savings. Mario, the exchange student from Italy with the curly brown hair, had said sagely, "You should do what you want right now because you might only have a year." And you had all agreed with him. But you didn't believe that, not really. You believed in continuity; you believed in the permanence of your own life.

You didn't go to Peru. You graduated with a degree in art history. You became a receptionist in a fine art gallery. You wore long white blouses, kitten heels, red flowers in your hair. You worked your way up the ladder; you went to parties and laughed at the right moments. You got married. You paid back your student loan just in time to get a mortgage. If you had known it would end here, on a curve in the road on Highway 3, you think you would have been different, you would have worried less, savoured the moment.

Drawn down through dark soil, where clumps and root hairs brush against you like the silvery threads of a cobweb, you struggle against whatever pulls you. Certain you are dying now, you're afraid of where you might be going. You want to be in the air again, with the road. You bargain. *Let me live. I'll give up all my petty concerns. I won't obsess about being four pounds over my ideal weight. I won't covet my neighbour's Beachcomber 750 hot tub. I won't complain about Saul leaving his dirty socks in the living room. I get it now. I get it.*

Your father took you to the Treasures of the Tomb of Tutankhamen exhibit when you were eleven. Inside the glass display case, you saw the funerary goods: a collection of pottery bowls, combs, gold bracelets and terracotta shabti—little figurines believed to wake and slave away in the Fields of Yalu for Tutankhamen in the afterlife.

"Why did the Egyptians think they could take all this with them?" you asked, your hand resting on the cuff of your father's anorak. There would be no need to brush your hair or roast a chicken after death. Your father, a professor of biochemistry, lived his life by the scientific method. He had impressed upon you a thirst for proof.

He leaned down to your level. The individual hairs that made up his beard became distinguishable.

"Honey," he said. "The Egyptians found it too scary to accept that death was final. Life was easier this way."

"That's dumb," you said. "What a waste of time making everything in the first place." And you went to look at the Golden Mask.

You were a collector. Desk drawers full of ticket stubs. Handbags you didn't use any more but couldn't bear to give away. Shoeboxes in the basement stuffed with vacation snaps. Close-ups of sweaty faces, out of focus, red and peeling. Over-exposed sunsets. Saul saw clutter as clogging the arteries of the house. He wanted ruthless practicality.

"Why don't we just throw it all away?" he said. "You don't even know what you've got. You'd never miss it."

But you wouldn't throw anything away because in the future you would arrange the photos in albums, in the future you would sit down at the kitchen table with a glass of wine and peruse them. You could have a slide show and invite your friends over for dinner and a viewing. Of course, you never did. You too thought you could take everything with you, all your treasures burial goods, talismans that promised an ever-lasting life.

You tangle in a root hair. It reminds you of swimming in the ocean, the kelp slapping against your legs. You never liked being in the water alone. Around you molecules pass through the root hairs' semi-permeable surfaces, and they sweep you along with them into the cytoplasm. You are liquid now, and the process hurts less. As you cross through the cortex cell walls and into the xylem vessels, you understand for the first time what it is like to be easy-going.

On the walk home from the Tutankhamen exhibit, your father caught your arm and stopped you on the sidewalk under a big elm tree. "The Egyptians didn't bury their dead that way just because they were scared. A good man spent his spare time making his own burial goods. He liked to do it. It brought him joy."

Rising up through the xylem, like a milkshake inside a straw, you're effervescent. You see now you wouldn't have lived anything differently. You couldn't have.

Up above, low pressure in the leaves draws new water molecules towards the stomata from the xylem vessels. As these water molecules move, they tug on others behind them, the pull transmitted from one water molecule to the next. You embrace the pull now, you lean in, you flow up. As you cross out of the xylem, you feel curiously like celebrating. You're going to miss the Earth, everything: running to catch a bus, drinking coffee in the starkness of a museum cafeteria, the colour of the sky in the fall, that far-off sort of blue.

"Yes," you say. "I accept it all. I accept."

You evaporate out of a spongy mesophyll cell into the space between, and in the intercellular gap, you can't remember your name. The leaf's stomata open, and you're transpired into the air. Now that this has happened, you're not ready. You don't accept anything. You rage against it. *No, no, no. I don't want to go.* You try to hold on to the narrative of yourself, but you're diffusing.

"I am..." you say, but nothing comes. Instead you catch glimpses: the skin on the inside of your mother's wrists, the taste of your own mouth in the morning, the sensation of laughing. Particles collide. You—

Lena Reynolds Gets Divorced

"I've met someone else." Mike's muffled voice came from the car phone, but he could have been calling from a submarine.

Lena said nothing. Late afternoon sunlight spilled through the kitchen window and set the glasses in the dish rack twinkling.

"Well, actually. I didn't just meet her. It's been..." He paused. "A while, but I can't do it anymore. It's making me ill, all of this lying." He sounded accusing as if the lying were somehow Lena's fault. The line wavered. "I want to be with her."

Lena hung up. She walked into the living room and stood in the middle of the carpet behind the couch, and then she turned around and walked back into the kitchen. She dialed his number again.

"I don't believe you," she said. She could hear him fumbling with the headset.

"Lena, please." His voice was small in her ear, almost timid. "Don't make this any harder."

"Say you don't love me." Why were these words coming out of her mouth? This was ridiculous.

"I don't love you."

She felt the world briefly shift on its axis, as if everything almost swung out of orbit. Fir trees and skyscrapers sucked into space. Lena rested her elbows on the kitchen counter beside the sink.

"How can you do this? Say good-bye to me this morning and take our kids to school and then call me at three o'clock and say it's over?" A carrot peel had stuck in the drain. She tried to unhook the clump with her finger. "How long has this been going on exactly?" She needed the facts. If she had the facts, this would begin to make sense.

"Two months."

"Months?" Lena had difficulty forming the word.

"I'm sorry."

"Why?" Her voice took on the same plaintive tone the children used when they couldn't have any more sugary snacks, a mixture of outrage and desperation.

"Because I care about you."

Was he crying? Her thoughts were foggy. She pressed her palm against the ridge of her nose. "No, not why are you sorry, why are you leaving?"

"This isn't the right time—I don't think that this…" He exhaled. "I'm not happy. We're not happy."

Lena ignored his use of the plural. She would fix this. He would articulate the problem, and she would do something about it. She turned on her take-charge voice. "What are you not happy with?"

"You won't talk me out of this. This isn't fixable, Lena." He sounded tired.

"You don't know that. How do you know it can't be fixed if you don't tell me what isn't working?" She would apply herself, the way she had applied herself to every other problem in their lives, logically and tenaciously. Lena The Reliable, The Responsible, The Super Reasonable. She'd been president of every club she belonged to in high school. She'd been Head of Administration at the local college before she became a full-time mom. Her friends dialed her number first in the middle of the night when their lives came loose at the seams.

"We want different things," Mike said.

She almost laughed. "Are you reading off a cue card? That's a bullshit platitude, and you know it. If you give me something specific to work on…"

He made a hum-hawing sound in his throat as if he were mulling over the reasons, coming round to her point of view, but then he said, "This is part of the problem."

"What is?"

"You can't let anything be. You try to control everything."

"I'm sorry I can't be more spontaneous about the end of my marriage." Lena hung up on him again. She shut her eyes and held her fingers against her eyelids. This was a mistake.

Last night they'd watched an episode of *CSI*, a show Lena had never really liked. She'd fallen asleep with her glasses on and woke up to Mike removing them gently from her face.

"Hey, sleepyhead," he had said lovingly, and Lena had halfway sat up to kiss him before she rolled over and went back to sleep.

Mike didn't come home that night, and he didn't answer his phone. Lena called him eighteen times. His phone didn't even ring but went straight to voice mail.

"Where's daddy?" Tom asked at the dinner table.

"He's working late." She looked down at her silent phone on the place mat. She couldn't believe he wouldn't call her back. "Dean, help Tom clear the table." She tousled Dean's hair. She tried to be bright and ordinary so as not to upset them. She went, smiling, into the downstairs bathroom and shut herself in. She didn't turn on the light. She felt comforted by the dark, shielded by it. This was the right place to cry, but the tears wouldn't come. She looked at her phone glowing in her hand. She dialed Mike's number. Her finger hovered over the call button. *Be reasonable. Stop torturing yourself. Mike will call you back. He has to process this too.* She pushed down hard on the call button anyway. She couldn't help herself. The pause before his answering service cut in was so full of promise she wanted to live in that moment. Then his recorded voice spoke into her ear. She pressed her forehead into the wall, the bathroom tiles icy against her skin. Leave a message, Mike's past self instructed her. *Leave a fucking message.* Lena had already left ten. She hung up before the tone.

Their bed felt strange without him. She slept fitfully. She woke once in the middle of the night from a dream that Mike was dead, her cheeks wet. She rolled over and gathered her knees into her chest and cradled herself. Don't overreact, she told herself. Of course, she would cope. She would make it through this. She let go, and her feet slithered into the cold space at the bottom of the bed.

In the morning, she dressed in her best jeans and an oversized grey sweater. She curled her hair. She dropped the kids off at school and kissed them both on the forehead. She waved at mothers she knew. She went to her volunteer shift at the food bank and to the grocery store. She took the bag of mushrooms out of her cart because only Mike ate them. She put a packet of Doritos in.

On her way home, she decided that information—guidance—was the way to handle this problem. People had travelled the path ahead of her. She drove to Chapters, circled the block twice before she found a parking spot. The self-help section was larger than she remembered. She chose eight books on separation and divorce. The cashier wouldn't make eye contact.

At home she left the groceries in their bags on the counter and took Marmite for a walk. She purposely left her phone behind on the kitchen table. She told herself she wanted to be present, but really, she hoped that if she didn't have the phone with her, Mike would call. He didn't call.

"Where's Daddy?" Dean asked as he came through the door from school, dropping his Batman backpack on the welcome mat.

"Working." Lena picked up the backpack. "He's very busy."

The day after that, she cleaned out the garage and took the broken weed whacker and the half-used paint cans to the dump. She dropped off Mike's old ski stuff at the thrift store. She put up a pegboard and hung up all of his tools. He had been promising to organize the garage for months. Still Mike didn't call.

"Daddy'll be gone for the rest of the week," she told the boys when they came in the door from school. "But he'll be back. It's only work stuff." She smiled and shook some chocolate chip cookies onto a plate for them. They both held out their hands.

That night she couldn't sleep. However she lay in bed, her body ached. She'd never had insomnia before. She sat on the couch with Marmite and tried to read magazines. At 3 AM, she signed up online for an aerobics class and a spin class at Women's Fitness, ordered a pair of $100 yoga pants and joined a single mothers' support group at her local community centre.

On Wednesday evening, Lena invited her sister Millie round after the boys were in bed.

"Are you two definitely done for good?" Millie passed her a glass of white wine and sat beside her on the orange sectional Mike had insisted they buy. Lena had wanted something that would age more gracefully.

"I don't know." Lena set the wine glass down on the side table untouched. "But we, *I*, have to think of the children. There's no reason this has to be dramatic."

Millie tucked her feet under a cushion. "Sometimes it's better to be a little dramatic."

"What's that supposed to mean?"

"This is a breakup, there's bound to be feelings."

Lena reached for her wine. "It's been a shock of course, but I'm not the first woman to be left by her husband and I won't be the last. This happens all the time. I won't fall apart over Mike, it's not practical."

"Pretending you're fine is never helpful," Millie said.

"I'm not pretending. I'm shocked. I said I was shocked. I'm not going to weep and carry on." She didn't add, "The way you would."

"Okay," Millie said, but it sounded like No.

"We all have different ways of handling things."

"I know that."

Lena wanted to curl up and be held. She was so tired. "I don't need your judgment right now. I need your support." The words came out sharper than she intended.

"I'm not trying to hurt you." Millie scooted down the couch and wrapped her arms around Lena. Lena pushed her face into the hollow above Millie's collarbone.

"It's going to be okay," Millie said. "You're going to be okay."

Mike showed up at home five days after his announcement.

He wore a suit Lena had never seen before. The steely grey fabric brought out the green of his eyes. Lena had been married to Mike for eleven years; she knew his body more intimately in some ways than she knew her own, and yet, standing there, he was a stranger.

"How are you?" he asked, his voice full of tenderness.

Lena hoped he couldn't tell how much that hurt.

He laid his briefcase on one of the kitchen chairs and crossed the space between them. "I'm sorry. I love our children, and I'll always love you, but our relationship was dead." He looked at Lena as though he expected her to agree. She stepped back towards the fridge. She had been hoping that he would take it back, tell her it was all a crazy mistake, apologize, kiss her.

"I'm fine," she said. "I think we should explain about her to the children together. I want them to know exactly what's happening and why."

Mike rubbed the underside of his jaw, and Lena saw the band of pale softened skin where his wedding ring had been.

"I'm not going to tell them I'm seeing someone else right away. It's too confusing. I don't think they should meet Valerie yet." He helped himself to an apple out of the fruit bowl on the counter. He took a bite and a fleck flew off and landed on the floor beside the table. Lena bent down and picked it up. The piece of apple stuck to her finger, and she had to flick it into the compost under the sink.

"Are you not sure about her?" She kept her tone spokesman-for-the-government neutral. "Is this a mid-life crisis?"

"Jesus, no! We've moved in together. But I want to make

sure everything's working before introducing our kids into the picture. The transition needs to be handled sensitively. First the kids need to accept our separation. I've done the reading."

He'd done the reading. The left side of her jaw ached, and she massaged the tightness.

"Is this how you want it to go or how she wants it to go?"

"It's what we want. She really hopes this can all be amicable."

"We all do." *We.* The new non-exclusive personal pronoun almost stuck in her throat.

"I'll grab the kids from school." He picked up his keys and briefcase.

"She'll have to be a part of their lives," Lena called after him.

He didn't answer.

"You can't keep us separate, and I'll have to meet her first. It's only right I know who the kids are with."

The front door shut behind him.

Valerie. She was 25, 12 years younger than Mike, and a receptionist at his firm. Lena found her employee profile on the company website and couldn't stop staring at her photograph. She had red curly hair and a warm good-natured face. Lena recalled speaking with her once at an office function a few years ago. She was nice, funny even. Was that what Mike saw in her? What else did she have?

On Monday evening, Lena drove across town to the Save-On-Foods near Mike's new condo. Ignoring empty spots closer, she parked a long distance from the entrance. She turned off the engine and sat in the car. *The Grown-Ups Guide to a Healthy Divorce* had forcefully warned on page 27 that going somewhere your ex-partner might be, with the hope of seeing him or his new girlfriend, constitutes stalking and no one, absolutely no one, likes a stalker. Lena put both hands on the steering wheel and flexed her arms. Valerie wouldn't definitely be grocery shopping here, it was just a possibility. Besides, Lena needed to grab some juice for the boys. She got out of the car and walked within ten meters of the automatic doors before she stopped. What if Valerie recognized her? Would she go up and say, "Hi, I think you date my husband?" She needed to get a grip on herself. Mike had moved on, she had to move on too. She went back to the car.

Mike came around to see the boys on Saturday afternoon, and Lena went to Starbucks for two hours. She was business-like with him, polite and unavailable. She bustled him out of the house at 5 PM when his visit ended.

"I've contacted a lawyer about how we'll divide the property and to calculate what I'll need in spousal and child support," she told him at the door. She wouldn't allow him to set all the terms of this breakup. He couldn't have everything his way.

Mike ran his hand through his hair. "Of course, you'll get half of everything." He seemed surprised by her brusque tone. He looked at her as if she were insinuating something unpleasant about him. "I'll pay whatever the boys need. You know I would never fight you for that. You deserve it."

"My lawyer'll be in touch," she said.

Mike glanced at her sideways. "Whatever you want." He walked out to his Range Rover and opened the driver's door. "I really want this to be harmonious. I don't see why it shouldn't be. We were always good friends."

Lena rested her shoulder against the door jam. Mike was wearing the Crocodile Dundee tee-shirt that she had found at Value Village about five years ago. The Wonder from Down Under, it said in fading blue letters across his chest. The neck had stretched. Did good friends betray each other? Did a good friend sleep with someone else for two months and come home at night and kiss his good friend on the mouth as though nothing were wrong?

"Good night," she said.

On Tuesday evening, just before the boys' bedtime, Tom lay on the couch, one arm dangling towards the floor as he watched cartoons. Dean had fallen asleep on the carpet, his legs scrunched into his chest. Lena went into the kitchen. Yesterday's dishes filled the sink.

A Lego pirate and his Lego pirate ship had run aground beside the garbage disposal. A brown stain dirtied the floor near the fridge. Lena bent down and picked up the pirate.

Her throat constricted, and she felt the scratchy urge of longing, the kind she used to get when she craved a cigarette. She wanted to talk to Mike. She straightened the pirate's arms and legs and set him upright on the counter. There's no point, she told herself, there's nothing you can do but get through this.

Tom had started to sing along to the Sponge Bob theme

song, his timing off, as if the television had an echo. Lena placed her hands on the counter and looked at the phone. Tom's voice strained for the high notes. The kids couldn't be left in this limbo. They needed routine. They needed their father. This couldn't go on. Sorting out a temporary custody agreement was essential. Lena moved to call Mike's cell but changed her mind. He was so lax about answering it these days. She dialed his new home number.

"Hello?"

Her voice. Lena held her breath, pained and thrilled at the same time. She wanted to hear Valerie, to see her. *Know thy enemy.*

"It's Lena." Her tone was flat. "Can I speak with, Mike?"

"Oh!" Valerie took a breath. "Of course, sure, I'll get him."

She heard Valerie call for Mike. Then Valerie's voice lowered, and they said things to each other Lena couldn't hear. She pressed her ear against the receiver. Was Mike the same man with Valerie as he had been with Lena? Did he call her cutie? Did he kiss her on the forehead?

Mike came on the phone. "Hey, is everything okay?"

She felt a rush of pleasure on hearing his voice, the familiarity of its timbre. She wanted to lean into the sound, be immersed in it.

"I realized I forgot to discuss the temporary custody agreement with you earlier."

"Uh," Mike said. "Can you hold on?" Lena heard him cover the receiver with his hand and say something she couldn't make out, then the sound of a door shutting and the faint noise of traffic.

"Look, as I said before I really want to take this slow."

"I get that, but it's confusing for the boys to spend only a few hours a week with their dad."

"Okay, I'll make an effort to spend more time with them, but I don't think they're ready to meet Valerie yet."

"I agree." Lena paused. "I don't think it's right that they stay over with you and Valerie. It would be too overwhelming for them." In the other room, Tom had stopped singing. Mike remained silent. The traffic in the distance hummed on. "So I think it would be best if Valerie moved out. We could set up joint custody then. You take them for the weekends, and in a year or so, when the kids have transitioned, you and Valerie can take stock of your relationship." In the ensuing silence, Lena bent down and picked up the Lego pirate boat and put it on the counter.

"I think the current set up is best for now," Mike said finally. "We'll organize a more permanent custody arrangement soon, okay?"

"Really? Because it seems like this is best for you and Valerie. You're a father first, Mike."

"I promise I'm going to find a way to make this work for all of us. In the meantime, I'll spend more time with them, okay? I'll organize a child minder so you get some down time too. I really don't want this to be harder for you than it has to be." He didn't wait for her to answer. "Good night," he said and hung up.

Lena put the phone on the counter. She drummed her clenched fists against the edge of the sink a few times. She longed to break something, do damage. She turned around, and her foot jerked out and kicked the garbage disposal. The bin shot back into the wall with a bang and the lid flew open. Lena caught it before anything spilled. She rubbed the spot on the wall where she had scratched the paint. "Everything's fine," she called out to the boys. "Mommy knocked something over, but everything's fine."

"Mike doesn't think the kids are ready to meet Valerie," Lena said to Millie. They were walking briskly around Elk Lake. Patches of pink sky shone through fir branches as the sun set. "And I agree, but at the same time, he's determined to keep living with her, which makes it impossible for us to work out a temporary custody agreement. He's acting like a spoilt child." Lena took her gloves out of her jacket pocket. "I suspect Valerie's threatened by the kids. I wouldn't be surprised if she's convincing Mike that being a four-hour dad twice a week is good enough because that's better for her."

The last rays of sunlight struck the water and turned the crests of the waves amber. Millie slid her hands into the sleeves of her fleece. "Mike loves his kids, you know that. I can't imagine he would let Valerie come between him and his sons."

"You say that, but by choosing to live with Valerie, he is. He can walk out on me, but he can't walk out on them. I'm this close to depositing them at his condo for the weekend and refusing to take them back."

"Hmm." Millie pursed her lips and looked out across the lake.

"You know I wouldn't actually do it."

"Hmm," Millie said again. "If I were you, I would have a lot of anger towards Mike. Some part of me would want to hurt him. You know, mess up his life a little."

"I don't want to hurt Mike, I'm not vindictive." A blast of cold air blew open the collar of Lena's jacket. She tugged the zipper up higher. "There's nothing I can do about it. He fell in love with someone else. I have to make the best of this situation. Move on."

Millie said nothing and kept her eyes fixed on the water.

The lake was dark now, blue-black against the deepening sky. Lena could see the car park at the end of the trail. "The most important thing is that this doesn't negatively affect the boys," she said. Her tone sounded righteous even to her. She changed the topic. "Did you hear back about whether you got that promotion yet?"

"Unfortunately, a much more male person was promoted above me once again." Millie turned to her and smiled.

"That's too bad," Lena said without feeling.

"I've got somewhere I have to be this evening," Mike said on Sunday when Lena came back from killing four hours at Hillside Mall. "But I'll make sure we talk about the custody stuff this week, okay?"

Lena scooped Dean off the living room floor and hugged him. "Okay," she said. Mike had a five o'clock shadow. It made him looked younger, rugged. She caught the scent of his aftershave.

He kissed Tom on the head. "See you later, boys." The front door shut behind him.

Lena smiled at her sons. "I'm going to grab some snacks, okay?" She went to the kitchen and came back with a plate of apple slices that she set on the coffee table. Tom drove his Tonka truck in a circle around the rug. He parked the truck beside the couch and came over to the table and grabbed a fistful of apple slices.

"Are we not Daddy's real children?" he asked.

"Tom! Where would you get such an idea?" Lena felt light-headed. She sat on the couch and pulled Dean into her lap. Tom snatched more apple slices off the plate with his free hand.

"Cause he doesn't live here anymore."

"Your daddy loves you," Lena said. "I love you, both, very much, and you're our real children. We just want to live in different houses."

Tom lowered his fist from his mouth, a string of drool extended and snapped back against his thumb. "Okay."

"Come up here and give us a hug," Lena said, and Tom dutifully clambered up on the couch and put his arms around them. A bit of half-sucked apple slice got caught in Dean's hair.

Her parents had the boys for the night. Lena had considered going bowling with friends, but Mike had said he'd call around 7 PM, and she wanted to find all the documents the lawyer had requested without the kids constantly distracting her. At 8 PM, when she had all the paperwork ready to go and Mike still hadn't called, she tried him. Voice mail. Her message was terse. "Waiting on your call."

She tried to tidy the boys' room, but she couldn't focus. How could he do this to her? She called again at 8:30 PM, no answer, then at 8:50 PM. How could he be unavailable? He didn't get to opt out of parenting. 9 PM. It wasn't fair or right. He should answer her calls. 9:05 PM. She was the mother of his children. 9:10pm. She couldn't take any more; she got in her car and drove to Mike's condo.

The building was new, with glass frontage, and a lobby finished in rough concrete and metal. Fake succulents in wicker baskets lined one wall. Mike had always wanted to live in a heritage-listed house. Places with memory, he said, not somebody's get-rich scheme. Lena hesitated and then pressed the buzzer hard.

Mike stood in his robe at the door when Lena came up the stairs. His legs looked thinner. "What's going on? Are the kids okay?"

"No. They're not okay."

"Where are they?" Mike stepped into the hallway and closed the door behind him.

"They're with my mother. They're fine. I only meant they're not handling the separation well."

Mike looked confused. "This isn't a good time, Lena. You can call me tomorrow."

"I've been phoning you all night." She stepped towards him. "We need to talk right now."

"You need to calm down," he said.

"I am calm. I'm just very concerned about our children."

"I'm not discussing this now, go home." Mike stepped back into his apartment and shut the door.

Lena stood looking at the brass numbers screwed into the wooden door. The ice machine by the stairs began to hum. He wouldn't get away with this. She knocked.

"Mike!" She knocked harder. "Mike!" She slapped both hands against the door until her palms hurt. The door of the apartment across the hallway opened, an older lady in a multi-coloured sweater stuck her head out.

"You're being very loud," she said.

"I'm sorry." Lena picked her handbag off the grey-carpeted floor. "I'm leaving now."

In her car, Lena felt clammy. She couldn't believe she had made a public scene, yelling in Mike's hallway in the middle of the night. Who was she? God, she hoped Valerie hadn't heard it all. How humiliating.

When she arrived home, she called Mike again to smooth over what had happened. Make things right.

"I'm sorry for overreacting," she told his voice mail. "But imagine hearing your son ask why his dad doesn't love him. And knowing that his father is on the other side of town, happily choosing another life and ignoring his family? It broke my heart. It's hard for me to see our sons go through this. I want to get the temporary custody thing organized because this negatively affects the boys. Please apologize to Valerie about the disturbance for me."

Lena sat on the couch and wrapped herself in the quilt her mother-in-law had given her and Mike as a wedding present. The call hadn't made her feel any better. If only she could speak to Mike, she could iron this out. He would see it from her point of view. She dialed his number. Voice mail.

"Hey," she said. "Sorry to keep calling, but I wanted to add that I'd really appreciate if you could call me back by tomorrow afternoon. That's not an unreasonable thing to ask, Mike." She hung up. She put the phone on the floor and turned on the television. A *Friends* rerun looked comforting, so she settled back into the couch.

A strange soft light fell through the French doors and turned the beige carpet a vivid turquoise. Lena stood up and went to the doors. Was someone in the garden with a lantern? The light hovered around the birdbath and then disappeared, leaving the garden dark. Lena stood for a few moments, confused. Was it a reflection from the street, or the kids next door messing around with a coloured torch? As she drew the curtains, the ball of light reappeared beside the garage. The light pulsed, dimmed to blue and then flared turquoise again.

Lena gripped the door handle. She wasn't afraid, exactly. It wasn't standard practice for house invaders to perplex their victims with a light show first. She had the same unnerved feeling she got sometimes doing laundry alone in the basement. She knew nothing was there, but she still felt watched, wary. Marmite stood up in her basket beside the couch and began to bark. Lena started at the noise.

"Quiet!" she reprimanded Marmite, but Marmite kept barking, her head lowered, and her hackles raised like a hyena. Lena tried to grab her by the collar, but Marmite wouldn't be held. She dragged Lena back towards the French doors and clawed at the glass, barking and whining. Lena left her and went into the kitchen to get a closer look. The back door out of the kitchen looked right onto the garage. She left the kitchen lights out so anyone out there could not look in and see her. The strange light beside the garage expanded like a fireball and went out again. In the other room, Marmite yelped and then fell silent. The light didn't reappear. Lena heard a car slow on the street. She exhaled. There must be a rational explanation for this. She went back into the living room. The French doors were wide open, the bolt still extended, popped loose from the notch in the lock. The curtains lifted in the breeze. Lena grasped both door handles and yanked them towards her. She leaned forward into the dark.

"Marmite!" she yelled. "Marmite!"

She thought she heard the click of Marmite's claws against the paving stones of the patio, and she stepped out into the garden. As she did, the entire back lawn lit up as though by a searchlight. Tree branches batted against each other.

Lena looked up at the disc shape above her. At first she thought it was a helicopter, but the machine made no sound. She heard Marmite yelping, but she couldn't see her. The searchlight went out and left Lena flash-blinded. Bright spots swam in her vision, and she stumbled backwards. As her eyes adjusted, she made out a shape hunched over by the birdbath. She tried to call out, but her throat was dry and tight and nothing came. The shape straightened up, it was too tall to be Marmite. Lena got down on her knees, as though by being closer to the ground she could hide from the figure. Shadows appeared along the fence line.

Get up, Lena ordered herself, get up. But she didn't move. She just knelt there, staring at the figure until a beam of light fell on her and she turned her face up. The world checkered into black and white as she floated upward. She flailed and tried to grab hold of something, to anchor herself to the earth, but her fingers found only air.

Lena came to lying on her back on a table in a cold circular room with a metal floor. The room had the antiseptic smell of an operating theatre. She felt drugged; one part of her mind asked, *Where am I? What's going on?* repeatedly, like a song stuck in her head. But she felt numb, anesthetized, until a warm sensation spread upwards from her stomach. She looked down at her own torso, now naked, and felt a sharp pain underneath her ribcage. Something was inside her. She writhed on the table. A force applied to her shoulders held her still. She turned her head and saw a metallic hand. Its three fingers pinched her skin. Lena looked up the length of the arm. The long-necked creature wasn't human. The face had no eyelids. Lena opened her mouth.

The TV blared. The clock on the DVD player read 01:11 AM. Lena lay on her stomach on the couch. She rolled over and sat up. Her head hurt, and she felt something moist on her top lip; she wiped it off with the palm of hand. Her nose was bleeding. Marmite, in her basket beside the couch, looked up at her, soft-eyed.

In the upstairs bathroom, Lena held a cotton ball to her nose and tilted her head back and looked at herself in the mirror. Her hair hung in limp strands. She threw the bloodied cotton ball in the wastebasket and turned on the shower. She peeled her shirt off. A red mark in the shape of a rectangle on her stomach and lower ribcage caught her attention. She examined it. Inside the rectangle, a few red squiggly lines angled out. Maybe she had fallen asleep on the remote control. She leaned back against the shower wall, shut her eyes and let the water caress her scalp and face until a stabbing pain pierced her abdomen and she gasped. The image of a circular metal room flashed to mind. With shaking hands, she switched off the shower.

She went downstairs wrapped in her towel; wet hair clung to her back and neck. Marmite stood up in her basket. Lena didn't know what she was looking for. The remote control was not on the couch or on the floor or even on the coffee table, but on top of the DVD player. She didn't remember putting it there. She looked around. The pile of magazines sat on the arm of the couch. The quilt lay scrunched between the couch cushions.

Lena stood in front of the television and told herself to calm down, to not jump to conclusions, to be reasonable; there was no one else here. But she couldn't shake her uneasiness. The house was too quiet. She listened for any sign of someone else. In the silence, the ticktock of the kitchen clock grew louder. Then she remembered. Of course. She'd been in the garden. She'd seen something beside the birdbath, and there had been that strange ball of light. She tried the French doors. Locked. She squatted down and looked at the bottom panel of the door. The wood was scuffed and scratched. She couldn't remember if it had looked that way before. She leaned back on her heels and rested her palms against the bottom pane of glass and looked over at Marmite. Marmite wagged her tail.

Lena couldn't sleep; the red mark on her ribcage was inflamed and itchy. She went to the bathroom for some chamomile lotion. When she bent down to get the lotion out from the cabinet under the sink, she felt faint and had to sit down on the floor. *This was all stress related. She was going through a divorce. The body reacts in surprising ways to stress.* She needed rest. She rooted around for the sleeping pills Mike had been prescribed a few months ago when he'd injured his shoulder. She'd feel better in the morning.

Lena woke before her alarm. In the dawn light, she rolled over and looked at her ribs. The mark had almost completely faded. She got out of bed and opened the curtains and looked out into the garden. The lawn was white and glittering with heavy frost except for a big circular patch about a metre from the birdbath where she could still see green grass. Lena caught her breath. She pulled her sweater on over her pajamas, stuck on her slippers and went downstairs. At the French doors, she hesitated, afraid, but she called Marmite, and they went out into the garden together. Lena wrapped her arms around herself in the cold air. Marmite ran ahead and sniffed at the patch on the lawn. Lena squatted down and touched the grass; dry, not even dewy. She pressed her palm against the ground. It felt no warmer than the frosted parts of the lawn. She stepped back and looked along at the fence line. The cherry tree nearest to the birdbath had flowered, the blossoms outrageously pink against the grey November sky. The other two cherry trees remained bare, their branches naked and spindly. Dazed, she walked over to the tree and stretched up to brush her hand against its flowers. They felt waxy to her touch.

Lena sat at the kitchen table, her coffee getting cold in front of her. Each time she convinced herself it had all been a stress-induced dream, she looked out into the garden and saw the tree, weighed down by blossoms, and her mind recoiled. If nothing had happened, why was the tree in bloom? She walked over to the window. The tree had lost most of its blossoms already. They scattered across the garden. Little flashes of pink. Lena peeled her shirt up and looked at her ribcage and stomach. A thick black, rectangular bruise, ringed by green and yellow skin had replaced the red marks, as though she'd been tattooed. She pressed the centre of the bruise with her index finger. It didn't hurt. Under her finger, her skin turned flesh-coloured and then blackened again, like a drop of ink diffusing through water. Lena sank to the floor beside the window. Nothing made sense anymore.

Mike answered on the second ring, his tone short. "I got all your messages. I'll call you this evening."

"It's not about that." Lena's voice wavered. "I think there was an intruder in the house last night, and now the cherry tree has blossomed in the yard and—I'm really afraid. Can you come over?"

Mike cleared his throat.

"I'm not making this up. Please, Mike."

"Fine. I'll be right there."

Most of the blossoms were already gone, a few browning flowers lay at the base of the tree. The bark had grown dry and brittle. The tree was obviously dying. Mike touched its trunk.

"It's just diseased, Lena," he said. "It needs to be cut out."

Lena looked at him, waiting.

"It's odd that it bloomed first, but that doesn't mean anything."

She crossed her arms and looked at the dry birdbath. A sprig of blossoms lay in its centre. "There was all this light in the garden, and Marmite went berserk." She didn't finish. She thought about the face without eyelids, the metal room. How would she describe that to Mike?

"Probably some kids playing a joke," he said. "I know you're having a hard time right now, but I can't come over every time a tree dies."

Lena stared at the birdbath. "I need some space for myself for a few days. Right now the boys are with my parents, but perhaps you could take them for the rest of the week? Valerie could go and stay with friends? Only for a little while."

Mike shifted his weight from one foot to the other. "Valerie thinks you're making a big deal of the little things because you're angry with me and you want to get to us." He rubbed his forehead. "That's not what you're doing is it, Lena?"

"Fuck you. I don't think your girlfriend should be passing any judgment on me."

Mike looked pained.

"I don't know why I expect something different from you. My parents will take care of the kids. And you can continue living a life of bliss or whatever the fuck you two are doing." Lena started back towards the house.

Mike followed her. "This is not forever, Lena."

She didn't turn around.

"I know you think I'm stalling because this is better for Valerie and me. But honestly I want the boys to get used to this slowly. I want to introduce Valerie into their lives in the best way I can."

"You chose this. These are the consequences of your actions. You can't expect me to take care of our children while you're happily ensconced in a love nest across town." She opened the kitchen door with more force than she'd meant to, and it banged hard against the wall. Mike put out his hand and stopped the door from slamming closed again.

"I know that. And I'm paying for a child minder. I'm seeing them three times a week, and I'm helping you with as many school runs as I can, and eventually, Valerie and I will take the boys half the time." He stood in the doorway and looked down at her. "I know I don't have the right to ask you this, but please, be patient with me. It's going to get better." His eyes radiated softness and concern. "I'll call someone about removing the tree."

Lena lay on the couch and stared out at the garden. The pale evening light washed the colour out of the trees. The bruise on her ribcage throbbed. She covered the mark with her hands. Her skin burned. She closed her eyes and saw herself lying naked on her back in the circular metal room. Her body bucked on the table. A second pair of three-fingered hands held her legs down. *We don't want to hurt you.* The words came from inside Lena, like her own internal monologue. *This isn't about you.* Lena flailed. She screamed, and a cold hand covered her mouth. *It will be easier if you let this happen.* Her body sagged and flooded with pain. The feeling filled up every part of her, and then the sensation dissipated. She felt light. Cloud wisps caught in her eyelashes. She saw the Earth from above, a shining, blue gem, and her heart sang to see it.

Lena sat up to darkness. She went to the French doors and peered into the shadowy garden but saw nothing unusual. She stood with her palms resting against the glass and watched the trees move.

In the deserted Elk Lake parking lot, Millie jogged on the spot. In the cold air, her breath came out in little puffs. She made a windmill action with her arms. A walker and a black Labrador disappeared into the trees at the head of the trail. Lena propped her foot up on the bumper to retie her lace, and then they set off.

"Has anything shifted on the custody thing?" Millie asked. Lena shook her head. There were patches of ice in the grooves of the trail. She looked out across the lake. In the clear winter afternoon, the water twinkled.

"Something weird happened to me the other night," she said. Could she say it? Her fingers rubbed the left side of her ribcage. The bruise had vanished.

Millie looked at Lena expectantly, her cheeks pink from

the cold.

"I think I got abducted by aliens." She recognized the absurdity of the words. If Millie had said that to her, she'd have laughed.

"What?" The right side of Millie's mouth curled up. "That's a crazy analogy right? Otherwise I'll have to get you committed."

"Forget it," Lena said.

Millie raised her eyebrows. Alongside the path, the wind moved through the undergrowth, parting bushes the way an animal would. Lena remembered the sensation of leaving the ground. Her body had arced backwards as though suspended by water.

"Really, forget I said it. Of course, I didn't get abducted by aliens. I'm being an idiot." If she continued this way, she'd end up on the corner of Douglas Street, in an oversized coat, proselytizing to the passing buses.

"So it's an analogy?" Millie looked confused.

"Something like that."

"Well, I'm not surprised you feel that way. You're going through something huge."

Lena remembered the sharp pain of metal under flesh. The pinch of fingers.

"I am," she said. "I really am."

Millie looked sideways at her. She hooked her arm into Lena's. "It's okay to go a little crazy from time to time."

Lena nodded. The lake came into view again; a silver disc against the sky.

Mike dropped the kids off when Lena got home from her

walk. He had taken them to the petting zoo.

"A baby goat ate a lady's scarf," Tom said as he clambered out of the back seat. Dean covered his mouth with his hand and laughed. Lena stood in the doorway as the boys ran past her and into the house. She wanted Mike to come in too and sit at the kitchen table with her and talk about his day. She wanted to make him laugh. She wanted him to brush the hair out of her eyes and kiss her. He waved and walked back around to driver's side of his Range Rover.

"Mike," Lena called. He turned around to face her. "I don't want to turn into your crazy ex-wife. I know I've been difficult. I'm hurt. This hurts. I'm trying."

I know," he said. His voice softened. "I appreciate you for saying it. I'm…"

They stood looking at each other. Lena longed to cross the space between them, to reach out and cradle the side of his face.

"I've been thinking that the boys and you should meet Valerie next week. Maybe for a walk or something?"

Their moment of connection was severed with Valerie's name. Through tight lips, Lena said, "It's a busy week next week. We'll have to see."

"Okay. We'll play it by ear." Mike got into the car.

Lena wished she could untie the little knots inside her. Before he shut the door, she said, "I can't promise anything, but I'll try to make it work."

He nodded. "Take care, Lena," he said, and he drove away.

The sun had disappeared behind the trees. She left the front door ajar and stepped out into the driveway. Stringy clouds blew by. On the horizon, she saw a strange light zigzag across a patch of sky, illuminating the clouds in brilliant blue and yellow flashes as it drew closer. She'd never seen a plane do that. *Probably the landing lights of one of those fantastically huge airbuses, that's all.* She stared at it for a few seconds longer and then went back into the house.

Snow Bunny

Paula and Judy were having cocktails before joining their scuba diving class for dinner, and they had the resort bar all to themselves. Paula was talking about the conflict in her office again. Something about how the receptionist wasn't relaying calls and had been caught lying about it and how Paula's boss wanted to give the receptionist the benefit of the doubt but Paula knew the woman was lying.

"Mm-hmm," Judy said, not really listening as she admired the sunset, rich with colour, almost tangerine. She'd never seen anything like it, but then she'd never been farther from home than Thunder Bay. She'd won this trip, two tickets for an all-inclusive one-week vacation at a five-star resort in Jamaica. She had never won anything before now. When a representative from *Food 'N' Style Magazine* had called to let her know, she had even asked the man on the phone to repeat it; she'd thought the call might be a scam.

Judy looked out behind Paula and across the white sand beach to where the sea darkened and turned inky against the sky. A couple walked along hand in hand. The scene might have been on a postcard.

"Of course, he's probably going to convince them it's all an innocent mistake." Paula slurped at her margarita. "He thinks with his penis."

Judy nodded. Her luck had changed. Winning this trip was a sign that life would be different. It wasn't that her life was terrible; only that it had stalled. She was 42 and unmarried. Love had never worked out for her. Her mother said this was because she had a terrible romantic streak and that her fantasies of how life should be got in the way. But Judy had tried. Life wasn't all about effort. In the end, love came down to chance, and she'd been unlucky. She had never met the right man. She worried now, not about accidents and bankruptcies, but about missing out on the good stuff. Of living a half-life.

"I'm dreading getting back to it all. Aren't you? How we will bear it after this?" Paula tried to unchunk the part of her margarita that was frozen at the bottom of her glass. She stabbed at the ice. Her straw bent ineffectually. A spray of margarita arced over the bar counter.

Judy laughed.

A young black man crossed the patio and weaved through the empty tables towards them.

"Hello, ladies." His accent lilted. He put his elbow up on

the bar, and Judy noticed a trace of salt on his skin.

"We're fine," Paula said. "We're not interested."

"Paula!" This was Judy's second piña colada in a coconut. She held her hand out to the man, and he took only the ends of her fingers.

"Beautiful, beautiful," he said shaking his head. "I'm Demaine. Do you like Jamaica?" He gestured behind him vaguely. Judy looked over his shoulder. In the growing darkness, she could make out the froth of breakers.

"It's paradise." The breeze stroked her bare back, sent a little shiver across her shoulder blades. Demaine released her hand. He sat on the edge of the bar stool beside her and rested one foot on the rung of her stool, his legs turned in towards her. The bartender came over and wiped around their drinks.

"Is everything all right?" he asked.

"Fine," Judy said. Her cheeks flushed under her slight sunburn.

"Whaa gwaan yaah mi breddah?" Demaine said. "Can I have a Kingston?"

The bartender didn't look at him. He went on wiping the entire length of the bar, lifting up each coaster. He walked back towards them and chucked the rag into the sink. He opened the beer fridge, slid the Kingston across the bar to Demaine and disappeared through the swing doors into the kitchen.

Demaine wiped the mouth of the bottle with his sleeve and took a sip. "Where are you ladies going tonight? How would you like to see the real Jamaica?"

"We've already got plans," Paula said. She didn't turn her head. She spoke to the frosted glass behind the bar, to the row of liquor bottles.

"I think we can miss one group dinner." Judy kept her tone deliberately light. She smiled at Demaine.

Paula stood up. Bits of coconut husk from Judy's piña colada scattered across the bar top. "Can I talk to you?"

The bathroom door shut behind them, and Paula leaned back against it. "What are you doing? Never mind that you're almost twice his age, he's a total sleaze."

Her lips pressed tight with disapproval, the same face she made when the Book Club vetoed reading *Eat, Pray, Love*—not even because they didn't like the book, but because most members had already read it, some more than once. Judy turned away from Paula towards the mirror. The walls of the washroom were overlaid with bamboo, the colour too beige to be authentic. She touched a section beside the sink to be sure. Plastic.

"I'm trying to do something different. Have fun, be spontaneous." Judy rested her shoulder against the wall. The hand dryer beside her brayed into life.

Paula opened her mouth to speak again, but she couldn't compete with the dryer, so they stood a minute not talking. Judy noticed how Paula's lilac dress strained against her upper arms, how the buttons gaped a little at her breast. The thickening of middle age, she thought, that settling that takes place.

"Do what you want," Paula said when the dryer stopped. "But I'm going to the dinner."

Judy looked at the blonde streaks shot through her hair by

the sun. She wore her best black dress, low-cut, sleek against her hips. Her tan was deep and even. "Will you be angry if I go?" She glanced back at Paula standing beside her.

"Why would I be angry?" Paula's voice came out thin, as though she were holding her breath.

"We came here together, and now I'm going to..." Unsure what she was setting out to do, Judy didn't finish.

"If you want to go, go. It isn't a big deal. It's not like I don't know anyone at the dinner. I'll be fine." Paula folded her arms. Her mouth said one thing, and her body said something else.

"I'll see you later, then."

In the mirror, Paula gave her the slightest of nods.

The lamps came on, and yellow pools of light fell on the boardwalk. Palm fronds brushed up against each other. Warm air touched the exposed skin on Judy's arms and on the backs of her knees. An older couple walked ahead of them on the path. The man had a flashlight, and he read from a guidebook as he walked, his legs luminous below his shorts, and as he passed each lamp, she could make out the blue of his veins.

"The bar's nearby," Demaine said. "It's a short walk, but we can take a cab if you'd prefer?"

"I'd like to walk. It's a lovely night."

"It's a very lovely night." He looked at her appreciatively, his eyes dancing.

Judy felt a little quiver of delight, pleased to be looked at like that, but she made a disparaging sound. "Pffft! I suspect you pick up tourist women at resort bars all the time."

"No!" He matched her with a show of false outrage and

gave her a hangdog look.

She shook her head at him, but she smiled.

"Are you American?" he asked as they passed the older couple. "From New York?"

"No, Canadian."

"Toronto! I'll come and visit you."

"Not Toronto," she said. "A small town."

"Still, in Canada. I think I would like it there."

"It's very cold." Judy mock-shivered and Demaine laughed.

"That's why you came to Jamaica, to warm up, and I'll come to Canada with you to cool down."

Judy forced a smile. "What do you do, Demaine?" she asked.

"I'm a musician. I have an album. But right now I play piano at the resort bars for the money."

"Wow!"

Demaine shrugged. "Jamaica's not an easy place. Not like in Canada. My dream is to leave Jamaica for a tour, but it's hard to get the visa." He caught her arm to alert her to a broken slat on the boardwalk.

The touch of his hand was light and cool. She stepped over the hole. "I hope everything works out for you." She looked up at the stars. She'd never seen the Milky Way so clearly, like looking at a creek bed full of shining pebbles. "Jamaica's so beautiful. You never see the night sky like this where I live in Canada."

Demaine looked up at the sky briefly.

Judy made her voice bright. "I'm a teacher. Elementary school."

He nodded.

"It's rewarding work. I feel like I'm part of something good, you know, helping shape the lives of children."

Demaine nudged her with his elbow. "But tonight we won't talk about work, we'll have a good time, huh?"

The path came out onto Main Street. Cars parked haphazardly, and groups of people swayed into the road amongst an incessant drone of drunken voices, like coming upon a beehive. Demaine led her across the street towards Rum Runners, a big sprawling bar. A table of American college boys smoked cigars on the patio. Dub music played so loud the speakers crackled.

Judy paused at the door. She had pictured something sophisticated. She'd imagined long discussions, lingering glances, glasses of wine, accidental touches.

Demaine responded to her hesitation and turned towards her. In the spotlight, she saw the fine web of wrinkles at the corner of his eye and the sinews, stringy, in his neck. He seemed troubled and tired, and for a moment, she wanted to comfort him. Place her fingers at his temples, try to draw the worry out, but instead she let him put his hands on her hips and guide her through a pack of gyrating girls towards the bar. He shifted her into the corner nearest the cash register. Through her dress, she felt the heat of his hands.

"Do you like Blue Lagoons?" He spoke into her ear.

"What?" She turned to face him so she would hear him. Her cheek grazed his chin.

"You'll like it," he said. "It's a Jamaican specialty."

Demaine pressed an aquamarine drink into her hand. His fingers found the base of her back. She had started to sweat, and her dress stuck to her skin.

"Let's dance." His breath was sour. He pushed her into the crowd.

Demaine danced as if the music started in the soles of his feet. Beside him a younger girl twisted and writhed, her belly taut beneath her pink tank top. Judy caught sight of herself in the mirrored wall, her body lumpy under her dress. Her hair, flat and wispy at the ends. Demaine reached for her hands to get her to dance with him. The strobe light freeze-framed his changing expressions. Suggestive. Sexy. Wolfish. She shook her head at him. She swung side to side, her movements heavy, belaboured, as though she were fastened to the earth.

"I'm going to the washroom," Judy said when the song changed. She wanted to be somewhere no one looked at her.

After the darkness of the club, the washroom's neon light stung her eyes. Judy abandoned her foul-tasting Blue Lagoon beside the sink. Two skinny girls in the line-up levelled baleful looks at her, and then went back to chewing gum. Their hoop earrings swung and caught light in rhythm with their masticating jaws. From under a stall divide, a dirty rivulet meandered around clumps of wet toilet paper. Thumping music swelled in the washroom like a wave.

Judy wished she were back at the resort. She thought of the restaurant with its fresh flowers and white linen curtains pinned back to let the warm night in and of the soft-spoken waiters who came to tend to her with the authority and carefulness of nurses. She ran her thumbs along her brow line. This had been a stupid idea. Perhaps the dinner had not yet wound down and she could still make it back to the resort in time.

Her head ached, and her new silver sandals felt too tight. The braided strap of her sandal strained against her little toe, where a blister had formed. She bent down and pushed her finger into the bulge; let the pleasant tingling pain fill her. The same sensation as biting into something sour.

When she came out of the washroom, Demaine was dancing with a girl in a white dress. He wasn't touching her, but his hands hovered around her hips and ass. She thrust her breasts and shoulders towards him, and the end of her ponytail flicked against his face.

Judy touched his shoulder. The girl in the white dress moved away and started dancing with someone else. Her hips rolled.

"I'm going home." Judy had to shout it into his ear. She drew back.

Demaine clutched her hand. "I understand. This is not for you. You need somewhere quiet for a classy lady." His breath hot on her ear.

Judy thought of the hotel room and of climbing alone into the immense bed, the cold, pressed sheets tucked in too tight. The air warmed between Demaine's palm and hers.

"Okay," she said. "Somewhere quiet."

He took her to Jolankees, a local bar off the main strip, thatched and dimly lit with no walls, so the sea breeze blew through like a change of mood. In one corner, a three-piece reggae band played with a concentrated inwardness, as if for their own entertainment. Two younger men were engrossed in a game of pool. The light over the table made the skin on the taller one's bare shoulders shine when he leaned in to take a shot. Demaine got Judy a beer, and led her out to one of the tables on the patio. He drew out a chair and she sat down and lifted the bun off the back of her neck. In the low light, Demaine's face grew gentle. Judy stretched her legs out, and the pressure came off her feet. Little tremors of relief travelled up her calves. Demaine reached across the table and stroked her forearm. His nails were clean and spade shaped.

"Tomorrow you can meet my little sister," he said. "She lives with me since my parents died. I have to pay for her to go to school, for her uniform, for her books, for everything. It's very hard for me to manage. My hope is to send her to university."

Judy looked over at the bar, to where the bartender spoke on his cell phone. His free hand picked at the wooden beam beside him. Demaine brought the beer bottle up to his lips and took a sip. The bottle glowed amber.

"I'll borrow my friend's truck tomorrow, and we can all go to a waterfall I know nearby."

"Maybe." Judy drew her feet under her chair so their knees no longer touched.

"I'll pick you up at the resort at 10?"

"We'll see," she said. She longed for some kind of kinship, to be seen and understood.

"The afternoon is better for you, maybe?"

She waved her hand at him to cut him off, a little drunk. "Are you happy with your life?" she asked.

Demaine smiled uncertainly.

"You know, is this how you imagined it would be?"

"I suppose so." He looked at the pool table. One of the men had sunk the white ball.

"Isn't life strange?" Her voice was sing-songy. She felt as though she were on to something, as though she were profoundly connected to the universe. She felt expansive. She wanted him to join in. "I always thought adulthood would be an arrival, that I would get it all, but instead it's just been a series of disappointments." She laughed.

He laughed too.

"Isn't it terrible when you realize things might never happen for you? Things that as a teenager you took for granted, like having children, getting married, being happy."

He nodded, smiling at her.

He was always smiling at her. She wanted him to tell her something meaningful, to dazzle her somehow. She pressed him, "Do you think we do it to ourselves, make up these fantasies about how life should be? Or do you think it's just one big lie they feed us to keep us complacent?"

He didn't answer.

She tapped her fingers against her beer bottle a few times. "I suspect we do it to ourselves. Just mindlessly believing everything we see on television."

"Sure," he said.

Judy slumped back in her seat, unsure why she felt so angry with him. Under the streetlights, the palms and blue mahoes appeared orange and unnatural. A long silence stretched between them. A few times, Demaine made a noise in his throat as if he was about to speak and then changed his mind. Judy covered her face with her hands. He got up and moved his chair round to her side of the table. The legs scraped against the concrete floor. He put his arm around her.

"Please, don't be sad, Judy." He tried to peel her hands back, but she wouldn't let him. He gave up and kissed her knuckles instead.

She pushed her palms upwards, exposed her chin, and his lips found her lips. She surrendered into the softness of his mouth. His tongue and teeth came up against hers, and she jerked her face down and then up and back, and the crown of her head caught him hard in the nose.

Demaine grunted in pain. He covered his face.

Judy stood up unsteadily. Demaine's hand splayed across his mouth and nose like a bandana. Blood oozed from between his fingers.

He wiped his nose with the back of his hand and then wiped his hand on the plastic yellow tablecloth. The blood coalesced, formed into droplets like water on an oilskin.

"I'm sorry," Judy said. The sight of his blood made her feel weak. "I should go. I'll be fine. I'll just get a cab."

"You're leaving me here?" Demaine's voice came out thick, clogging in his bloodied nostrils.

"It was an accident." She felt lightheaded.

"You fucking snow bunny."

Judy put her hand down on the table to brace herself.

"You want me to please you all night. Nothing is good enough for you. You think I'm just here for you, for your entertainment?"

She stared at him.

"Get lost," Demaine said. "I don't want to see you."

The veranda light for Judy and Paula's bungalow was out. Judy's key missed the lock twice before finding traction. She pushed the door open, wanting to not wake Paula, but her concern only made her movements more erratic. Her keys clinked loudly on the bedside table as she laid them down. She bumped against the bed on her way to the bathroom. Before she shut the door, the glow of the bathroom's overhead light illuminated the satin throw on Paula's bed. The chocolate the maid had left at turn-down lay undisturbed on the pillow. A black rectangle on a sea of white. Judy stepped out of the bathroom and turned on the main light. She looked around as if for evidence of where Paula might be at two in the morning. Was she really still out at the group dinner? None of their other dinners had finished this late. Judy sat on the edge of Paula's bed. Paula was not the kind of woman who got into trouble, she took care of herself. Still....

Judy rested her elbows on her knees. Her feet ached from those ridiculous shoes, and she sat, unmoving, working up the effort to get undressed and into her own bed. She reached over and took the chocolate off Paula's pillow and popped it in her mouth. It tasted like cardboard.

The heat of the room woke Judy. She felt the beginnings of a slight hangover; the dryness in her throat and a faint pulsing along her hairline. She pressed her tongue against the roof of her mouth. Paula's clothes from last night lay crumpled on her made-up bed. No sounds came from the bathroom. Judy got up and found a note wedged into the corner of the mirror above the vanity table. "At the pool."

Judy turned on the cold tap and lowered her face into the sink. She drank water out of her cupped hands and let it splash against her cheeks and neck. She examined her wet face in the mirror. Blue shadows under her eyes. Pinched skin around her mouth. A looseness along her jaw line.

In the shower, she squatted down under the spray, and warm water gushed over her, almost as comforting as being held. Afterwards, she lay on the bed wrapped in her towel. Her wet hair made the pillow damp, and she pressed her cheek into the cool, reminded of having mumps as a child, of the touch of her mother's calm and loving hands.

The day was stark, the sky endlessly blue and unruffled. She had forgotten her sunglasses in the room but felt too lazy to go back for them. She held her hand in front of her eyes and scanned the sunbathers beside the pool until she saw Paula, on her back, her yellow-and-white-striped sarong across her belly. Her pink painted toes curled over the edge of the lounger.

"What happened to you last night?" Judy sat down beside Paula, the sun-bleached canvas hot against the back of her legs. She had missed shaving a patch around her ankle. Stiff black hairs stood to attention.

"Judy." Paula pulled her sunglasses down on her nose like an eighties starlet. "This is Brad."

On the lounger on Paula's other side lay a large man in a pair of too-tight board shorts. His big red belly glistened. He was drinking a Mai Tai, and he held out his free hand to her. Judy had to lean over Paula to shake it. Her tote bag slipped down her arm and brushed against Paula's knees.

"You missed a good time last night," he said. "You should have come out with us."

"Brad's from Windsor," Paula said. "He's with our tour group."

"How nice." Judy arranged her towel, and lay back on the lounger. She shut her eyes. Red-coloured afterimages danced about behind her eyelids.

Paula and Brad talked about real estate prices in Muskoka. "Not as much as you'd think," Brad said. "A friend of mine got an amazing place for under three."

"Still," said Paula. "Think how many weeks you could spend here for that kind of money."

Brad made a non-committal sound.

"Really? You don't like it here? I think six weeks a year here would do me fine."

"I liked last night."

Judy opened her eyes. Paula cuffed Brad on the arm and laughed. From the patio above them, the lunch gong sounded.

"It's buffet time!" Brad said in a funny voice.

Paula laughed again. "Are you coming, Judy?"

"I'm not hungry yet. I'll be fine here." Judy took her book out of her tote bag.

"We'll see you later, then." Paula sat up to collect her belongings.

Judy let her open book rest on her face and listened to the shuffling sounds of Paula rolling up her towel and, in the distance, the regularity of the waves. The sun on her thighs felt blissful. She concentrated on that, ignored the feelings of regret and dread, the aftereffects, she told herself, of too much alcohol. When she peered out from underneath her book, Brad and Paula had gone. The entire poolside had emptied for lunch, leaving the loungers and umbrellas in disarray. The wind picked up, sent ripples skittering across the surface of the water.

A man rounded the far edge of the patio in bare feet, his cotton pants rolled up. He seemed to be moving towards her. She sat up a little and squinted into the light at Demaine and felt a rush of relief. He wasn't angry, it had been a drunken misunderstanding, and all this could be fixed. She waved.

He didn't wave back, and she dropped her hand. Demaine walked right up to the end of her lounger. His head blocked out the sun, and Judy felt the coolness of his shadow on her belly. She propped herself up on her elbows.

"Is your nose okay?" she asked. He stared down at her, and she tugged her sarong up over her stomach. "We both had a lot to drink. It was a stupid mistake." She smiled at him. She wanted him to absolve her somehow, though she hadn't done anything wrong.

"You think I'm nothing."

Judy shrunk from his venomous tone. "No," she said. Her voice trembled around the edges.

"All of you coming here to Jamaica to use us."

He loomed over her, and Judy struggled to sit up fully.

"No." Her voice became high-pitched and aggressive. "I know exactly what you were trying to do all night. *Canada this, Canada that, how hard it is to get a visa, blah, blah, blah.* Do you think I'm stupid?"Judy gathered her sarong around herself and stood up.

Demaine stepped back from the lounger.

This was pointless. She didn't mean him any harm. The anger went out of her. "Let's not fight about this. There's no need. We're both sorry. Can't we forget it?" She looked searchingly into his eyes, hoping for softness, for a reprieve, but his face was cold and full of dislike. He turned his back on her and strode out of the pool area.

"Demaine, please!" she called after him. "Demaine!" Judy sat back down on the lounger. She heard the other guests coming back from lunch, the rumble of their voices on the patio above her. Little spurts of laughter. She trembled. How dare he? How could he accuse her of using him? If he wasn't so touchy, they could have just enjoyed themselves. She had only wanted to have a nice time, to be desired. It wasn't about him. It had nothing to do with him.

She took her dress out of her tote bag and pulled it over her head. Why was he so angry? If he had just been willing to engage in a nice conversation, none of this would have happened.

Paula called her name and leaned over the patio railing. "We're going to the market in town, if you want to come?" The hem of her dress blew through the bars and she pushed it down against her thighs.

"I'll be right up." Judy slipped into her sandals and shoved her sarong into her tote bag. She wouldn't let a man as angry and rude as Demaine bother her. She would enjoy the rest of her day. Her luck would change, and everything would be different. She crossed out of the pool area and wished she had remembered her sunglasses; the brightness of the afternoon pained her.

Versus Heart

I met Joel at a dinner party at my sister Sheila's house. He was recently separated and older than me, forty to my twenty-six. We sat next to each other. We were shy. He passed me the butter.

"I think you're perfect for each other," Sheila said in the kitchen as I helped her make the coffee, the rest of them still in the dining room. She had a willow pattern milk jug in her hand, and she lifted it for emphasis as though she were making a toast.

"Who?" I asked. I knew exactly who she meant; I just wanted her to say it.

"Joel." She put the milk jug on the tray. "He's still getting over the separation. It's been five months, but she did leave

him for another man. That's always a shock." Sheila got the
sugar bowl out. "But he's lovely. Kind to women. Thoughtful. I
think you'll work. Could you get the dark chocolate out of the
fridge? Top shelf."

Sheila, Patron Saint of Lonely Hearts, always set me up. I
think she believed that the love of a good man would help me
be a better person because she said stuff to me like, "True love
does wonders for self-confidence" and "Before I met Michael
I was afraid to let someone get close to me, but once I did, I
really started living." And then she'd look at me out of the
corner of her eye to see if I was, you know, getting it. And I'd
look at the cat. *Here, kitty, kitty, kitty.*

Joel took me out to dinner. A sushi restaurant that could
have been any sushi restaurant: plastic menus, nondescript
furniture, a row of booths along one wall like carriages in a
novelty train. He ordered eel. I ordered avocado rolls.

"I need to take this slowly, Zoë," he said. "I just want to
get that out of the way."

I blew waves in my cup of popcorn green tea and avoided
his eyes. "I'm terrible with chopsticks," I said.

The waiter brought me a pair held together with elastic
bands. The supposed chopstick equivalent of trainer wheels.
I tried unsuccessfully to pick up the napkin. Joel laughed.
I wasn't sure about him. He didn't seem my type. I usually dated a loose approximation of a good man. The kind who
borrowed money, who could roll a joint one handed and still
wanted to be the lead singer of an indie rock band. My back
catalogue consisted mostly of beginnings. Damp matches that

flared and then fizzled out. The main players varied, but the plot arc always looked the same; the relationship started at full tilt, but I had a tendency to press the emergency eject button before take-off. Something about feeling close to other human beings triggered my gag reflex.

The sushi platter arrived. My handicapped chopsticks, unpincered, clasped only air.

"You're right, we should take it slowly." I stabbed the tip of one chopstick clean through a piece of ginger. Joel called the waiter over and asked for a fork.

After dinner we went straight home together. His place. A real house. Flower boxes. Hardwood floors. Kitchen equipment. A beagle named Solomon who had a bowl with his name engraved on it. Joel opened a bottle of Malbec. He put on Gillian Welch, and we sat on the paisley print couch. I still had my boots on. After the first glass of wine, he knelt down and took them off for me. He rubbed the back of each of my calves. He pressed his palms down softly on the tops of my feet.

In bed, he was measured. He explored my body. He took pleasure in his discoveries, the mole on the ridge of my pubis, the scar behind my knee from a tree-climbing incident. He kissed me between the legs, soft and probing, not the frantic tonguing I usually tolerated. This was slow. A steady downfall. The kind that makes a river rise. My body surprised me.

He drew the sheet over us, and we lay side by side staring at the ceiling.

"Did you live here with her?" I asked. "Was this your house?" I had seen no traces of her. I didn't really care. I was simply curious.

"Yeah."

I lived in a rented studio apartment above Impulse Foods convenience store. My landlord, Mr. Chong, let me paint the floors sky blue. It was a ten-minute walk to work at the Black Bean where I used my BA in Sociology to push Fair Trade coffee and vegan baked goods on office workers. It seemed so improbable that my life would intersect like this with a man who did real things like get married. I did unreal things like go to roller derby games and read comics about the zombie apocalypse. I felt like a tourist to his world, but I wasn't interested in the sights in the brochure, I wanted to see the seedy parts. I rolled over onto my stomach, and he put his hand on my back and stroked me absentmindedly.

"Did you see it coming? Her leaving you?" I asked. "Or was it a shock?"

His hand stopped moving. "A shock, but looking back I can see we had grown apart. It wasn't right any more. I'm glad we're over." He rubbed my back again, this time in concentrated, circular motions. "Let's talk about something else," he said.

I didn't care that he was still hung up on her. Being heartbroken gave him an edge that made me more interested. Otherwise he'd have been only a nice middle-aged guy with a dog. I'd met Her once, his first wife, ex-wife, at Sheila's wedding. She had been one of Shelia's bridesmaids. They'd become friends in university. Joel must have been her Plus One. I had only the vaguest memory of her. Her heel broke walking up the aisle, and she bent down and took off her shoes. She was laughing. We didn't look the same—she was thin, blonde, big-nosed—but we had similarities. We had both been ill as children; her with Reye's syndrome, which scarred her liver. I had rheumatic fever, which weakened my heart. In Chinese medicine, the liver is associated with bitterness, resentment and a tendency to fly off the handle. "When the heart is out of balance, a person speaks too fast or laughs inappropriately."

Joel drove me home in the morning. In the car park outside Impulse Foods, he took my face in his hands and kissed me, a good kiss. A tequila shot kiss. It burned all the way down. I saw Mr. Chong peering at us through the window, his mouth obscured by a poster advertising half-price luncheon meats, so I couldn't tell if he was shocked or impressed.

"Did I mention that my saliva's poisonous?" I said as I got out of the car.

Joel laughed. He leaned across the passenger's seat to look up at me. "I'll call you soon, okay?"

"Okay," I said.

We made dinner at his house. Fresh linguine, rolled flat and fed through the teeth of a pasta maker. Cherry tomatoes, basil, olive oil. I chopped garlic. He came up behind me, pressed his lips against the back of my neck. The knife trembled in my hand. A liquid feeling I couldn't name—something languorous that made me want to sink into a warm bath. My knees brushed up against the kitchen cupboards. He let go of me and set the mixing bowl in the sink.

I had a rule, it was *don't fall in love*. Most people heard that as if the emphasis was on love, but the part that was really important was the falling. *Don't fall*. Rappel down with a safety harness. Tell someone where you are going. Take extra water. Love is chemical. I've looked it up. Vassopressin. Oxyoctin. You are impaired by love. You shouldn't operate heavy machinery. Fatal errors have been made under the influence of love.

In the dining room, he dimmed the lights and lit a candle. He touched the top of my foot with his foot under the table. I looked down at my plate. The linguine slurped around the prongs of my fork like the tentacles of an octopus.

"Are you feeling shy?" he asked, and I blushed and swung my legs under my chair.

"No. It's that the mood in here is revolting. Are we going to go on a moonlit walk along the beach holding hands? Or slow dance in the living room to nothing but the beat of our own hearts?"

"Very unlikely," he said, softly.

The curtains opened. I didn't move.

"I have to go to work," he said into my ear. The smell of toothpaste and aftershave. He brushed the hair out of my eyes. "But you can leave whenever you want. Drop the key back through the mail slot."

I pulled the sheet over my head. A shroud. Made the noises of the undead. He laughed and kissed me. His lips made the sheet damp against mine. *Nothing but large and beautiful flowers, which parted from each other of their own accord, and let him pass unhurt, then they closed again behind him like a hedge. Sleeping Beauty opened her eyes and awoke.*

Without him the house was strange. I felt unwelcome. In daylight the kitchen could have been a two-page spread. Sun dappled. Apples in the fruit bowl glowed. The fridge looked fearsome, a hulking stainless steel presence. The contents of his kitchen cupboards were arranged as though catalogued. A museum of the modern man. Le Creuset pots and pans. Fig jam. I found the coffee filters tucked behind the glass jar of beans. While the coffee brewed, I went into his study. On the shelves, a smattering of books: *The Diviners*, Graham Greene, a guide to guerrilla gardening. I half-opened the top drawer of his desk, but I stopped. In Spyzone on West Pender, you can buy a pinhole covert camera for seventy dollars. A tiny unblinking eye.

"Easy to conceal in household objects," the clerk had said. Little pools of grease collected in the acne scars on his forehead. "Imagine all the monitoring opportunities." He took the camera out of my hand and turned it over in his palm.

"Imagine!" I said. "Though with your employee discount, you probably don't have to."

Flash To: Int. Dingy one-room apartment: an oil slick in the sink, a beige couch tattooed with cigarette burns. The girl in the fishnet stockings excuses herself, goes to the bathroom. By remote access, the pinhole camera in the empty shampoo bottle clicks on.

Cut To: Int. Spyzone on West Pender:

"I'll have to think about it," I said to the clerk. "I'm not sure I'm as ready as you to start incriminating my loved ones."

I looked around Joel's study for the camera's telltale glint. The give-away. I didn't see anything, but when you're up to no good, the question you have to ask yourself is not *Is this right or wrong* but *If they found out, would I care? Can I live with what I've done?* I opened the drawer. Last year's taxes (a gross income of fifty-eight thousand dollars), an unused pad of Post-it notes, his passport (in the photo he was surprised, the flash lifted the wrinkles from the corners of his eyes. On page 8, a stamp from Dubrovnik, Croatia. I couldn't make out the date).

Above the desk, a row of russet-coloured photo albums on the shelf, the physical manifestation of our generation gap. The first album contained family photos from the seventies. Action shots of kids in bell-bottoms riding tricycles. Close-ups of a garish, yellowed Christmas tree. Toothy smiles. The second album was all landscapes. Ontario in the fall. A green Ford Taurus parked on the side of a back road. Rain falling on a lake. Nothing to glean from either of them. Expecting cocaine, getting talcum powder. In the third album, suddenly, Her. A jolt. Her on a pink couch with her knees tucked into an oversized sweater. Her leaning over the railing of a ferry, the wind lifting the ends of her hair. Her looking at the camera, her expression gentle, unmasked, her eyes shining like abalone shell. She seemed so much more real than me. She took up space in the world. The photographs gave their relationship heft. I couldn't see how that would ever happen with me; I wasn't a person who ended up in someone else's album. I came and went without a trace. Some First Nations tribes believed a photograph could steal your soul and imprison it within the fusion of polyester, celluloid, salts and gelatin, leaving you to wander this Earth, spiritless.

I put the albums back on the shelf. It was sort of gross to be a part of this intimacy. I felt sullied. The coffee maker announced the end of its brewing with a series of gurgly coughs. I went back into the kitchen. His ex-wife had nothing to do with me. I poured a cup of coffee and sat at the kitchen island. I had nothing to be upset about.

After that She haunted me. I wanted not to care about her, but I didn't know how to make the feelings stop. I Facebook stalked her. Her security settings let me see only her profile picture and her date of birth. Aquarius. Erratic. Changeable. An extrovert. An Air sign, an Aquarius is high-minded and analytical.

I found her professional website. She was a Jin Shin Do practitioner. She promised to balance my "Qi" and improve my vitality. She called her clinic Shen Bodymind Healing. In Chinese, *Shen* means spirit, god, awareness. It can also mean a large shape-changing sea monster associated with funerals and mirages. I imagined making an appointment. I wanted to see her for myself, but I thought she would recognize me.

I lured Sheila to a La Vie en Rose outlet store on the pretense of helping her shop for bras and then asked her veiled questions. She offered nothing but platitudes.

"They were well-suited," she said. "I always thought they'd make it. Wired or unwired?" She held up a pink push-up bra for me. I didn't answer. She lowered the bra, and her face softened. "I don't know what to tell you. She's a lovely woman, they just didn't work out."

"Unwired," I said. "They always end up that way anyway."

At dusk, in knee-high boots and a baby blue dress, I rode my bike out to Kingsway to meet Joel. Traffic swelled and ebbed around me. I felt heat coming off the cars. While I was chaining my bike against the lamppost outside Rodriguez, I saw Joel watching me through the glass. His eyes slapped up against me. Hair trigger.

"You look beautiful," he said when I sat opposite him.

I was hot underneath my clothes. There was something repulsive about being complimented.

"You shouldn't judge a book by its cover." My voice came out snarkier than I'd intended. Pincushion. Girl with a mouth like a coat hanger. He didn't laugh. The waitress brought two pints of Blue Buck. Water condensed on the glass.

"How was your day?" I asked him to make up for my lack of grace.

"Pedestrian."

I took a sip of beer, as he watched me. I tipped the glass right back, exposed the softness of my throat. I wanted to tell him that I had looked through his photo albums, that I spied on him. I wanted to ask him about her, but I didn't want to risk his anger. He ordered yam fries. I ate the parsley garnish, and we discussed:

1) How reprehensible it was that dentistry was not included in national health care. I told him a co-worker had a terrible toothache and had to go home early. He told me he'd knocked a tooth out as a child. That led to discussing:

2) Childhood humiliations. I told him about going to some-

one's house for a birthday party on the wrong day. The blinds were down. Her mother answered the door in a towel. A sour smell. The flush of her cheeks. He told me about not understanding that a kid in his class came from a poor family and asking him why he had such shitty toys.

The waitress brought us another round. I spun the beer on the coaster. "I watched a bunch of YouTube videos of failed marriage proposals today," I said. "Grand gestures met with pained refusals. Why would anyone do that? You're only asking to be humiliated." He didn't say anything. I looked sideways at him. "Oh, don't tell me you asked Her to marry you with the aid of a Jumbotron at a hockey game?"

"No."

"How did you ask?" It was like picking at a scab.

"I just asked. We went out for dinner."

I couldn't understand why he didn't want to dish the dirt on her. That's part of the delight of a new relationship: a colluding audience for the character assassination of your exes. You're supposed to revel in it.

"Was it a monster wedding?"

"No." He leaned forward, looped his hands around his beer glass. I leaned back. I wanted to say, tell me everything. Tell me all about it, but I didn't want him to think I was jealous or insecure, that I was threatened by her, so I said,

"Did you wear a top hat? Was there a poodle ring bearer?"

"I really don't want to talk about it, Zoë." He took a swig of his beer.

I ran my finger round the edge of the coaster, feeling like a pricked balloon, worried that he could tell. "Dan Mangan's playing at the Biltmore tonight," I said. "So I'm going to go."

He looked startled. The fingers around his pint glass flexed and then let go. I tried to get my arms into the sleeves of my denim jacket without standing up.

"Is everything all right?" he asked.

"Yup." I gulped down the last of my beer. He rocked the chair back on its hind legs.

"Am I invited?"

"Sure." I kept my tone light, easygoing. Frosting on a cupcake. I was pleased that he'd asked.

We lay in his bed. His fingers walked up my forearm. I thought of ants. He kissed the crook of my neck and then my earlobe.

"Do you think I'll ever meet her?" I hadn't meant to say it, but the words slipped out of me.

"Probably not. There's no reason to."

"Why don't you want to talk about her with me?" That feeling of being high up and on the edge. I teetered. Blood rushed to my head.

His voice became small. "It doesn't feel right."

I pulled my arm back.

His hand fell on the sheets. "I loved her, we were married, and now we're not. I can't tell you it was nothing because it wasn't nothing. She was the most important person in my life, but that's over now."

I felt a sharpness in my chest. My voice moved up a register. "I think it's weird that you're so secretive about your previous relationship. It makes me suspicious."

"Secretive is bit of an over-statement. I'm cautious about discussing her with you because I think it might be uncomfortable for you." He pulled me into his arms.

I lay rigid, full of dislike for him.

"If I'm honest…" He stopped and pushed his face into my hair. He started again, his voice full in my ear. "If I'm honest, it's also because I still feel a sort of loyalty to her."

It was as though he had hit me. A tight feeling that my body contracted around, and I wanted to push back hard against him. He reached over and stroked the soft skin on the inside of my wrist with one tentative finger, the way you might stroke a dog you didn't know. He looked into my eyes, and his smile said, *Don't be afraid, I'm harmless and well meaning.* It made me want to crawl underneath something.

"I should go." I sat up. "I have stuff to do." I held the pillow in front of my body. He sat up too and caught me by the elbows.

"I only feel that way out of habit," he said. "We were together so long, and this is all new. I like you. I like what is happening between me and you."

I got out of the bed and pulled on my jeans. I couldn't see my bra. I had to reach around him and look under the pillows, but it wasn't there either. He found it stuffed between the bed and the nightstand and passed it to me.

"I think you're making this into a bigger deal than it has to be," he said.

"It's not a big deal. I have stuff to do." I couldn't get my bra to clasp.

"You should stay, and we should talk about this." He scooted across the bed towards me. "Get back in here."

The bra clip found traction. I put on my shirt.

He changed direction. "I didn't mean to hurt your feelings. If you need some space, I get it. We'll talk about this another time, okay?"

"Sure, whatever you want." I had my back to him.

"Do you need a ride home?" He exuded such concern he could have been my high-school guidance counsellor.

"I'll be fine."

I shut the front door behind me. The night was cool. The air smelled of ocean, of underwater places. I zipped my purse into my jacket and unlocked my bike. I stood for a moment with the padlock in my hand. He didn't follow me out. I felt tart, acidic, ridiculous. I wanted to punish him. I got on my bike and rode downhill. Trees leaned over the streetlights. Their branches cast giant leafy shadows on the asphalt.

The next morning, I went out to breakfast alone at Solly's Diner on the corner. I felt as though I had sandpaper in my chest. Everything made me angry. The menu with its hipster puns, the way the sun fell through the dusty windows, how difficult it was to peel the lids from the tiny creamers. I doodled on the *Globe and Mail* and thought about doing outlandish things, like moving to Alaska and working in a fish processing plant or hitchhiking to Portland to become a burlesque fire dancer. I ignored two calls and five text messages from Joel, all of them a version of "Let's talk about it. Call me. I'm sorry you're upset, blah blah blah." Except for the last text where he wrote, "If you don't tell me what's going on, we can't work it out. I think you need to ask for what you want."

"Did you get that from a fortune cookie?" I wanted to text back, but I didn't. I didn't want him to know he had any effect on me.

"Do you mind moving to the counter to finish your coffee?" the waitress asked. "We've got a brunch rush."

"I'm leaving anyway." I stood up. I hated her. Her tattooed arms. Mermaids and albatrosses, a sailing ship, the coffin that slipped overboard and sank into the hollow of her elbow. I didn't leave a tip.

Joel didn't call all week. I checked my phone inside the bathroom at the Black Bean, next to the overflowing bin of paper towel and the graffiti under the mirror that said, "Joanie is fucking boyfriend fucker." Beside which someone else had written in ballpoint pen, "Get a boyfriend who doesn't want to fuck Joanie." A million bathroom breaks a day, until Ruby the shift manager asked if I had a bladder infection.

By Friday afternoon, I didn't care anymore. I was over it. *A large hedge of thorns grew round the palace, and every year it became higher and thicker; till at last the palace was hidden, so that not even a chimney pot could be seen. Many, many princes had tried to cross the hedge of thorns. But none of them could ever do it; for the thorns and bushes laid hold of them, as it were with hands; and there the princes stuck fast, and died a miserable death.*

Lois worked the same shift as me, and she came home with me after closing with a $10 bottle of Bonarda and a bunch of MDMA. There was a DJ at Crush that she wanted us to go and see.

Lois tried on a selection of my dresses, wriggling in and out of them. With one hand, she held out a silver minidress.

"Too short?" she asked. Her bra had greyed, and the straps were sort of yellowy. The elastic in her underwear had gone too, and they bunched up around her ass. Did the Fairy Godmother make over Cinderella's underwear too? Or was it only your outsides that magic took care of?

"If it's too short, you can borrow my electric blue booty shorts for underneath." I topped up her wine glass.

She raised her eyebrows and pulled the dress over her head. I stuck my feet up on the coffee table and rested my wine glass on my belly. My phone rang. It was Joel. I let it ring. Lois turned around from admiring herself in the mirror. She shimmered in the low light.

"Who are you ignoring?" she asked. The phone stopped.

"Just some guy." I went into the kitchen. I shifted the cutting board and a pile of unopened mail out of the way and sat on the table with my feet on one of the mismatched chairs. I called him back.

"Hey," he said. "It's nice to hear your voice. I've been worried about you. Are you okay?"

"I was in the shower."

"Okay...Did you want hang out tonight and talk about what's going on between us? I think we left things on a bad footing."

I wanted to say, "Yeah, sure, of course, I've missed you," but instead I said, "Throw in some popcorn, and it's the best Friday night ever."

"If you're not interested in this, just say so."

I slid off the table. "My friend Lois is here, and we're going out, if you want to come?"

He didn't answer.

"We'll have fun," I said.

"Okay." He sounded unsure.

I felt liquid. The whole world slowed down. Everything became much more interesting. Lois smiled at me across the table. Two of her flame-coloured dreads fell across her face, and she flipped them back over her shoulder like a pair of feelers.

"I want to move." She got up. She kissed me on the forehead on her way by. Joel shifted down the table towards me.

"I'm feeling a little old." He smiled at me for reassurance.

"You're fine. This crowd's very accepting of the midlife crisis."

He laughed and reached out across the table and touched my hand. I reverberated.

"Do you want to dance?" I asked.

We moved through the crush of bodies. I found his hand. Lois's caught me around the waist from behind. She peacocked into the centre of the dance floor. Joel swayed to the music, but he moved like he didn't quite mean it. I leaned towards him. He smelled of Old Spice and Tide detergent.

"I'm high," I said into the side of his jaw. My lips rasped against his stubble. I held on to his arms as though they were a ladder out of a pool.

"What?" he asked and pushed me away to look at my face.

"I'm high. Do you want a pill?"

He scrutinized me under the roving blue light. "Okay," he said.

We sat on a tatty velvet couch in an alcove. I flushed with sensation. The rushes ebbed and flowed. I felt like a flare star undergoing a striking and unpredictable increase in brightness. I wanted contact. In a binary system, a companion star can induce flares in another star when their magnetic fields become entangled.

"Are you feeling it yet?" I asked.

"I think so." His face was round and open as a saucer. I dangled my leg over his leg. Electrical discharge. A channel of ionized air between a cloud and the ground becomes the path of least resistance and makes for a stronger current from the earth back up. This is known as lightning's return stroke, and it is the most radiant. He eased back into the couch and put his arm around me. Our faces pressed towards each other.

"Do you like me?" I asked him.

"I really like you." He kissed me, his lips as soft on mine as whipped cream. The music throbbed. I moved with it. He cupped the side of my face, and I looked into his shining eyes. Schopenhauer says the weakest feeling of the sublime is in seeing the light reflected off stones. It is the pleasure of observing objects that are no threat. Joel's gaze wandered. I felt the loss of his attention as a sudden drop in temperature.

"I like you," I said, and his head turned back to me. His face opened up, and I folded into him.

"I'm threatened by her," I said into his neck. The drugs made me fearless. "I don't like that you were married to some-

one else. It makes everything between us seem so insignificant."

"I get that." The timbres of his voice made me resonate
like a drum membrane. His face came down to my level. He
exhaled, and strands of my hair blew across my eyes. His
jaw clenched rhythmically. Bruxism stimulated by the drugs.
It made him look moonstruck, intense, possessed. "There's
nothing I can do about the past. But I don't want her back," he
said. "I promise."

We looked at each other, and I wanted to hold the moment
like a long note, but he shifted away.

"Let's go dance." He pulled me to my feet.

We left before closing time, as the drugs wore off. After
the humidity of the club, the night was sharp, like a change
of season, and the city was empty but for nocturnal creatures,
the night bloomers. They called out to each other, jubilantly.
They collected in the doorways of 7-11s. They howled at the
big mama moon. Joel and I held hands the whole walk home.
He even opened his front door one-handed so he didn't have
to let go of me. I took my dress off in his kitchen and left it
beside the stove. As we walked to his bedroom, he leaned over
and kissed the tops of my breasts. We lay down sideways on
the bed. Our noses touched. The Inuit do not need to kiss each
other, nose to nose. It is not so cold their mouths form ice together, though at the North Pole spit freezes in midair.

"Did you have fun?" I asked. He nodded, and I kissed
him. "I'm really happy you came out."

"Me too," he said and he closed his eyes.

The sheet half slithered from the bed when I rolled away from him. I rose and went into the bathroom. I looked like a pirate in the mirror. Smudged eyeliner. Wine-stained teeth. The magic show was over. Time to go home. I got into the shower. He knocked.

"Ow. Ow. Ow. How's your head?" he said through the door. "Do you want coffee?"

"Sure." I did a forward bend. Held on to my toes. The uttanasana pose supposedly helps relieve fatigue and mild depression. I only felt dizzy. The water surged over my back. The door opened, and the shower curtain drew back. I straightened up. My wet hair clung to my forehead. He stood there looking at me appreciatively.

"What?" I felt shy.

He ran his fingers over my collarbone. "Nothing. I just thought you might be lonely."

He made coffee in his boxers. He turned around when I came into the kitchen. I didn't want to be looked at. I slid into a chair.

"Well," I said from behind my hair. "I'm sorry about the bizarre emotional malfunction last night. Good drugs. I guess."

He squatted down beside me and rested his hands on my knees. "I meant everything I said. I like you."

The tone of his voice made me feel as though I were made of honey. I turned my face away. "Where's my coffee? The service in this place is dreadful."

"It's coming!" He laughed and went over to the coffee maker. "I've some stuff to do this afternoon so it's going to be a quick breakfast, but we could have dinner later, if you like?"

He passed me the mug, and I put it to my mouth and looked at him over the rim. I had wanted to spend the day here with him. I felt rebuffed by his unavailability, and my throat tightened.

"I'm busy tonight," I said into the mug even though I had no plans at all.

"Okay," he said. "Dinner tomorrow?"

"Maybe." I wanted to hold him at a distance. I stood up. "I should go."

He came over and kissed the top of my head, but he didn't ask me to stay. He didn't walk me to the door. He didn't even say he'd call me.

I went out into the street. Droplets of rain misted against my hair. The world looked rinsed, houses bleached out by the grey sky. I stopped in the middle of the sidewalk. I really wanted to go to dinner with Joel. We could go for Thai, and I could wear my patchwork skirt. I went back up the stairs and stood on the cusp of his doorstep. Grand gestures. Pained refusals. I leaned across and knocked on his door. He opened it.

"Forget something?"

I looked over his left shoulder at the Mrs. Dalloway poster hanging on the wall. I almost said yes.

"No." I felt right up close against my own skin. I felt see-through. Sitting duck. So much easier to shoot than a diving, flying, dabbling duck. He looked at me.

"I don't have plans tonight," I said, my voice squeaky. "I said I had plans because you had plans this morning, and I know it's stupid and not your fault at all but that hurt my feelings and so then I wanted to hurt you back."

Joel rolled back on his heels. He seemed to be thinking it over. "Okay, crazy girl," he said finally. "I'd love to go to dinner with you. See you at 8?"

"Okay." I went back down the stairs. I could have skipped. *Twelve fairies came, each with a high red cap on her head, and red shoes with high heels on her feet, and a long white wand in her hand: and they gave all their best gifts to the little princess.* I crossed the road. Below me the city unfolded into Saturday afternoon. The wind caught my coat, tugged at it. I let it blow open. I felt the rush of cold air against the skin of my throat.

Gone South

Dear Shashi,

The biopsy on the peanut-shaped mole on my shoulder
blade came back positive for melanoma. Despite the fact that
the doctors kept assuring me that the odds were in my favour.
Nothing to worry about, they said. This seems to be the way
of the Doctor. They like to placate you and insinuate that your
concerns are misplaced, and then at the last moment, they like
to get you good and panicked. I'm beginning to think this is
a technique taught in medical school, probably on the same
syllabus as How to Speak Entirely in Impenetrable Acronyms
and The Importance of Bustling and Looking Unavailable.

In the past week, I have submitted to a barrage of scans.
They exposed me to cyclic sound pressure, electromagnetic

waves and x-rayed me, and the bad news is they found three more tumours burrowed beneath my scapula bone and a fourth lodged next to my sternum. This counts as metastasis. I have Stage IV melanoma. Don't look it up. I wish I hadn't. I've had a dark week, as you can imagine, full of hopelessness and self-pity. I barely got out of bed. I kept my face pressed into a pillow and grieved. I might not even turn thirty-four. Would I get to see the global warming skeptics eat their words? Would I see out the season of *Mad Men*?

Noah reminded me that I was not actually dying yet, that we're still no closer to knowing how this will end, and I have every reason to be optimistic. He's right. My doctor says that given my low level of metastases, with treatment the outcome could be reasonably good. I refused to ask what reasonably good means. Hopefully, it means until my mid-seventies. I have an appointment for next week for a treatment plan, and I've resolved to stay positive. I'm healthy, strong, and determined to fight like a lioness.

Yours,
Ruth

Dear Shashi,

Aside from the tumour on my shoulder, I'm showing no outward signs of illness. I'm going to yoga and running twice a week, and everyone keeps commenting on how well I look and so life goes on. I still try to subsist entirely on stilton and figs, Wingnut still won't play fetch with me despite my pleading (he's a no-good dog, but I love him), and I'm still enjoying my work at the Youth Counselling Centre as much as ever. I have

some great clients at the moment, resilient, funny, courageous
kids, and I'm grateful to be part of their lives. I'm lucky to do
what I love.

Most days I can't believe I have cancer. It must be a mistake, I think. How could everything remain so ordinary?
Standing in line at the bank to pay the hydro bill, spilling
coffee on my jeans, the way the sunlight strikes the cherry
trees and transforms the view from my window into a Polaroid
picture. I try to vanish into those ordinary moments.

My oncologist has recommended I participate in a com-
parative Phase Three clinical trial for a drug called Proleukin.
Because here's another fun fact about melanoma: melanoma
cells do not respond to chemotherapy; apparently they have
overactive DNA repair genes, so melanoma's generally treated
with immunotherapy rather than chemotherapy. Chemotherapy
is a toxin that wipes out all the rapidly dividing cells in your
body, while immunotherapy triggers your immune system to
produce its own T cells and natural killer cells, and then they,
hopefully, annihilate the melanoma cells for you. I like to
think of immunotherapy as the carrot and chemo as the stick.
Becoming a self-educated oncologist is one of the side effects
of treatment. The waiting room is full of cancer patients moon-
lighting as doctors.

I have to undergo a series of scans to see if I'm eligible
for the clinical trial. Noah's calling it *The Goldilocks Tests*,
because in order to qualify, I have to be just sick enough. Too
little or too much, and I'm counted out. Even if I qualify for the
trial, I won't necessarily end up being treated with Proleukin,
as patients are assigned at random to two groups: one treated
with Interferon, and the other with a combination of Inteferon

and Proleukin. I have a newfound admiration for the lowly lab rat, he who gives his life to medical science against his will.

The average success rate for Interferon alone is around 15%. The trial average for the combination therapy is about 25%. My oncologist made it clear that those statistics are not for curing or eradicating my cancer but only for stalling and shrinking the *existing* tumour growth. I wonder what the success rate was for bloodletting? Apply leeches liberally.

Obviously I want to get on the Proleukin arm of the trial. Those marginal percentage differences could mean life or death. Noah couldn't believe that I don't get to choose which drug I want. But I guess everyone would choose Proleukin, and then who would be in the control group? They'd have a dud experiment on their hands, and that would be the end of Medical Science. Apparently the end of Medical Science is much worse than the end of me.

Considering everything, I'm feeling hopeful, and tough and stubborn. I ain't going nowhere. I really think everything will be okay. I will be okay. Fingers crossed the trial goes my way, and this Big Ole Cancer-beating Show gets on the road soon. Watch out, Melanoma!

Yours,
Ruth

Dear Shashi,

The good news is I've been accepted into the clinical arm of the trial! I'll be one of the participants treated with Proleukin and Interferon. *Tell her what she's won, Ladies and Gentlemen!* An infusion of each drug twice daily for twenty minutes—four days on, ten days off—over three cycles, and then I stew in their juices for two and a half weeks. After that, some blood work and another scan to check if the drug is doing its job.

If I were a participant in a "blind trial," the oncologist said, I wouldn't know which drug I received, and if it were a "placebo blind trial," then I wouldn't know if they injected me with the drug or with "sugar water." That would be hilarious, if dying didn't hurt so much.

I've signed on the dotted line of a million waivers and consent forms, and they've drawn nine vials of my blood, and so my treatment begins in three weeks! Metastatic melanoma is incurable, so what I'm hoping for is stasis. No further tumour growth. However, the oncologist believes that if I contain the disease to the four small tumours in my soft tissue, I may survive for a long time. When he said that, I felt as though my parachute deployed. I cried in the stairwell after my appointment. I hadn't realized that I'd been living in free fall.

I had the tumour on my shoulder removed a few days ago. The result of the surgery is a jagged incision between my shoulder blade and my spine. It won't be a pretty scar, but Noah thinks it'll help me make conversation with strangers at the pool.

Oi, what happened to you, then?

Stabbed in the back.

Either way, I'm delighted the tumour is out of me, and I can't wait to get this drug trial started and shrink the rest of those mothertruckers!

Yours,

Ruth

Dear Shashi,

I'm on medical leave until I feel better. Noah isn't sure I made the right decision to quit work early. He thinks that I'll succumb to depression without anything but my disease to focus on. You know how he is, a man of constant activity, a devout believer in practicality. He thinks we should try to keep everything as normal as possible, but when I'm at work, I feel as if I'm being held between two pieces of tracing paper. Nothing quite touches me. I'm far off from myself.

I've been trying to enjoy life, and often I succeed. We've been out eating and drinking and seeing friends and living it up as much as possible. I've dragged Noah to the arts cinema several times and then forced him to discuss the movie with me afterwards over a glass of red wine. He's been good-natured about it all and calls it my pre-treatment uproar. He sends his love to you and his congratulations on Mike's promotion. I'm full of envy that you're moving to Paris. I will definitely visit once my treatment is finished. I can't wait!

Ruth

Dear Shashi,

A tumour has appeared on my right hip, visible just below the surface of my skin. It's a hard, strange lump, as if someone found a way to press a pebble into me. At first I thought it couldn't be a tumour because who has tumours appear on the surface of their body? Seriously, what am I? A dog? Is this dog cancer? I kept trying to rationalize. This is not a tumour because my body's fighting and winning this war. This is not a tumour because I'm so healthy. It's not a tumour because I feel fine. It's not a tumour because this *cannot happen to me.* But that's not how cancer works. You could be doing a hundred push-ups a day, and inside, your cancer has metastasized from liver to lungs. There's no rationalizing.

The tumour on my hip will stay put. My oncologist says given the spread of my disease, systemic malignant cell eradication will be more effective than individual tumour excision, and that if they operate now, they'll have to delay the immunotherapy until after I've healed. I wanted to beg him to cut it out of me. I'm tempted to hack it out myself. I cannot bear to see that little protrusion. I get dressed in the dark. I made Noah cover up the bathroom mirror. If I so much as brush my hand against it, I want to scream. Noah's insistent that my medical team knows what they're doing. He thinks they're refusing to remove the tumour because they want to maintain the integrity of my body and keep me healthy enough to fight. He keeps assuring me that the drug treatment will destroy all the cancer cells. But I suspect they won't remove it because they expect more tumours to appear. They can't keep chopping them out, or there'll be nothing left of me. I'll be a human colander.

Do you remember when we were 15, and you cut my hair to give me that bob with a shaved nape that was all the rage in the 90s, and the shaver slipped and I ended up with a runway halfway up the back of my head? I cried for days. I would go to the bathroom every hour and check to see how much hair had grown back in the last fifty-five minutes. I wouldn't let anyone see my head. I wore floppy hats to school. And then the chemistry teacher, Mr. Cochrane, made me take my giant hat off during a Bunsen burner experiment because it was a fire hazard. I was so in love with Liam Wright, and he sat behind me, and I could feel his eyes on that exposed strip of stubble on my scalp. I would have done anything to have my hair grow back instantly. I remember thinking that nothing worse could ever happen to me, *my life is over.*

I know all this rage and fear isn't helpful, and I have to stay positive and appreciate all the love and care in my world. I have to believe I will get through this.

My mother arrives tomorrow; she will take care of me through the drug trial period, as some of the side effects can be nasty. I've been exercising, and hydrating and eating well. I'm steeling myself for the fray, fueled on organic vegetables and yoga. I suspect I will feel better when the treatment begins and I'm actually doing something to combat this heinous disease.

Yours,
Ruth

Dear Shashi,

I had my first infusion this week. I sat in a giant leather recliner, swaddled in blankets with a heating pad across my knees. The chemo nurses administered Benadryl to counter any allergic reaction and Acetaminophen in case of fever. They rolled hot towels around my arms so my veins would vasodilate and inserted an IV in one wrist for the saline solution and an IV in the other for injecting the Proleukin. As soon as the drug entered my bloodstream, the flu-like symptoms struck, like being injected with winter. The icy sensation began at the IV site and travelled up my arm. I was wracked with shivers. My hands and feet turned Antarctic cold. A metallic taste filled my mouth, and then both my eye sockets pulsed and my sinuses burned. My bones ached.

I've finished my first cycle of doses now, and the side effects persist. Bruises from the needle punctures pucker the skin in the dips of my elbows, and my palms tingle as if with static electricity. I imagine if I touched you, your hair would stand on end. I've got a banging headache that follows me around like my own theme tune, and when I blow my nose, it comes out pink because my platelet count is so low. The oncologist assures me I will feel less mutant during the week without drugs. Either way, I have finally begun treatment, and I tell myself that I feel so ill because these terrible drugs are working!

Yours,
Ruth

Dear Shashi,

I believe the treatment is slowing my tumour growth. I'm scared to even type those words in case I jinx it. But my appetite has returned, and I even gained a couple of pounds. My mother says I'm looking healthy again, and Noah's being unbearably smug about the success of the treatment.

I've had a week off the drugs, and I've been making the most of this reprieve. Some days, I didn't think of my illness at all and went out into the world as a whole and happy human being. I went for a walk in the woods today and talked about books and ideas with a friend. I laughed without feeling a shadow over my heart. At sunset, the clouds turned the colour of peach ice cream. I felt buoyant, as if living is effortless, as if I were a stone skipping across a lake.

I'm hungry for experience. I want to run until my thighs ache, I want to ride around in the desert at night with the windows open, hot air licking the moisture from my skin. I want to smell frangipani. I want to come home from work with wet hair and muddy boots, and spend the evening watching *Real Housewives* and eating almond butter out of the jar. I want to live.

I'm afraid to get ahead of myself. As the oncologist constantly warns me, stasis is the most we can hope for, and that means I may never go back to a normal life, but who knows what is possible? Every day, I walk the tightrope between denial and despair. I think perhaps we do that all our lives, but only when you are ill is the tightrope brought into such sharp focus.

Yours,
Ruth

Dear Shashi,

I hate needles. I hate their thinness and how they shine. I hate how my skin flexes and bows to their pressure, and I hate how, when one is inside me, I still feel its rigid, metallic coldness. At my request, they installed a plastic IV tube into a vein in my chest. It's called a port-a-cath, and it makes me feel a bit like a robot. This won't be removed until the end of the treatment, so I don't have to be jabbed quite as much. The only downside is sometimes my port clogs, and I have to stand with my arm above my head and cough to shift the blockage.

If that doesn't work, the nurse flushes me.

I'm right in the middle of Round Three of the Trial, and so far, I have had fewer side effects than during the previous two cycles. Though every now and then, I'm beset with the odd shivering fit and the tiredness is worse. Some mornings, right after I've got out of bed, a wave of fatigue swamps me, and the effort required to bring my coffee mug to my lips feels daunting. Even so, this round is closer to the snuffles than a nasty bout of avian flu, so much more bearable.

The chemo room at the Cancer Agency has an open plan, and we all sit around together getting dosed. It's the saddest opium den in the world. Yesterday, I sat next to a forty-year-old mother of two with Stage 3 breast cancer. Her head was a hairless orb, white and dimpled as the moon. She drank orange juice through a straw and read *People Magazine* as though she were at the salon getting her nails done. A man about Noah's age sat in the corner by the window. He wore work clothes, stained Carhartts and his flannel shirt folded up over his elbows. He kept his eyes shut and his face to the wall. A drop of his seafoam blue cytotoxic drug splashed against his bare skin and scorched him. The nurse injected this drug into an IV in his forearm and pumped the poison through his veins and straight into his heart.

Yours,
Ruth

Dear Shashi,

This morning on CBC, I heard a woman talking about surviving a plane crash in the Arctic Circle. One moment, she sat in a climate controlled metal tube with wings slicing through the sky, and the next, she lay face down in the tundra, the wind whipping through her hair. A human foot, a miniature can of Coca-Cola and a plastic-wrapped ham-and-Swiss croissant landed beside her. She looked up to see a column of smoke rising from the fuselage. She lasted through the night by keeping a bonfire burning, fueled by the wreckage. She drank tiny bottles of whiskey and ate several of the deluxe cheese trays. She was too afraid to despair. Hope is not logical.

My friend Sally came to see me today. She brought me frosted lime cupcakes, and she was kind and thoughtful, and I hated her. It pained me to hear that she's going to Hawaii in two weeks. While she's lying on a white sand beach, daydreaming beneath her sunhat, I'll be at the Cancer Agency getting juiced. Even her problems with a co-worker only elicited my envy. What do problems with a co-worker mean to me? It's all so insignificant. I've been banished from the realm of the immortals.

I interact with Noah and my mother as if a vacuum lies between us. I've crossed over into some space they don't understand. My mother makes sure I'm comfortable, finds books for me to read and brings me endless cups of green tea, but she shuts down whenever I try to talk about the possibility that my treatment will fail. She can't allow herself to think of the future that might face me. Part of me is afraid to die because I don't want her to know that kind of unhappiness. I don't want to break her heart.

Noah tries hard to hear me. He lives with a therapist, he's a pro at reflective listening, but he keeps telling me that we don't know what will happen and to stay focused on the present. He holds onto my body in the night, feels the weight of me, and I am so solid to him, so real and so permanent, that he cannot conceive I might die.

I imagine this is how a war veteran might experience her homecoming. All around, life is ordinary. Your mother makes you a sandwich. Your husband brings you the mail. But you know you're out on the edges of your life, fighting a battle against enemies only you can see.

Please still send me all your news. As difficult as it is to hear about other people's lives, I still want real relationships.

Yours,

Ruth

Dear Shashi,

It's the middle of the night, and I'm experiencing a strange pain down the back of my neck. I burn and throb and tingle. I'm acutely aware of my body all the time now. Even sitting is uncomfortable. I'm fixed to my flesh and bone, no more flights of fancy, no more daydreams. I'm bound to this disappearing body. I've lost thirteen pounds since October. I'm practically skeletal, yet I subsist entirely on two-bite brownies and cherry supreme ice cream. My teenage self would be impressed.

Since last Wednesday, I developed mouth ulcers, and the skin on the backs of my hands is red and blotchy and itches like I've been bitten by a swarm of mosquitoes. I'm also suffering from orthostatic hypotension, and so intermittently, the act of standing up causes my blood pressure to plummet, which in turn causes me to plummet. Noah keeps asking me if I've been tight-lacing my corset. You would think with so much practice I'd be more competent and that as soon as the darkness closed in on the sides of my vision I'd simply sit back down again, but somehow it always catches me unaware. Coming to is a strange rebirth. I find myself rolled over by the stove or collapsed beside the toilet.

Noah's unflappable optimism exhausts me. He's convinced that my symptoms are no more than side effects of the drugs, rather than the effects of my cancer, and that once the trial is over, I will feel much better. I need to keep looking ahead and being positive, he says. Yesterday I asked if his arms were tired from banner waving. He walked out of the room. So I'm guessing the answer is No.

Next week is the CT scan. If the cancer has progressed, I will have to come off the Proleukin trial and begin another course of treatment. If I can't be cured, then I wish for amnesia or ignorance or to get run over by a bus. I don't want to look down the barrel of my own life. Can I not be spared that? Noah says that if I didn't know about my cancer, I couldn't do anything about it. But human beings are not designed for this. Death should be sudden and unexplained. It should take you mid-sentence on a hot afternoon with a drink in your hand.

Ruth

Dear Shashi,

I got the results from the bone scan. The bad news is that the melanoma has spread to one of my ribs. I'm sure the appearance of this new tumour will count as disease progression and I'll be booted off the trial. I'm still waiting on the rest of my results. On the bright side, the superficial tumour on my hip is no longer clearly visible and feels as though it has been pulverized with a blender. I imagine my insides to look like a game of Pac-Man. The power pellets have given me the ability to eat up Inky and Pinky and Clyde, but those pesky ghosts keep getting re-spawned. Still, if I get ten thousand points, don't I get a bonus life?

I'm becoming intimately acquainted with despair.

Yours,

Ruth

Dear Shashi,

I had hoped to spend this week pretending to be a perfectly ordinary thirty-three-year-old woman. You know, a bit of restorative yoga, a visit to the mall, a sneaky glass of wine or two and perhaps a ramble in the woods with my dog. But my right arm, after years of good service, decided it would rather be a useless appendage. When I woke on Thursday and asked my hand politely to put itself down on the bed and help me get up, it wouldn't answer, and no amount of coaxing has worked since. My shoulder had been giving me a bit trouble for a while, due to the surgery I thought, but now I worry that I have nerve damage in my cervical vertebrae.

I've been for a scan and in a mere week we will know what is wrong. I don't understand why the operator of the imager can't just tell you what she sees. There's so much medical bureaucracy, as if they hope to muffle you under all the paperwork. I often feel like an afterthought, as though the technicians and surgeons and nurses hang about the hospital to do something other than make me well. The healthcare system could save millions by employing vervet monkeys to press buttons and move slides around.

Noah feels confident that my inability to grasp objects or sign my name is side-effect related. Proleukin can cause inflammation of the nerves, which can lead to paralysis. Either way, I am doing my best to get my arm working again. I don't want to panic, but it is difficult to experience such a sharp physical decline. I miss you, right arm. Left arm is valiantly filling in, but one-handed typing is slow.

Write soon and tell me everything.

Ruth

Dear Shashi

I'm on a lovely cocktail of Tramadol and Oxycodone, so I'm currently pain-free. What's more, I sleep, I walk around, I bend over, I sit down! Batteries not included. I've had radiation on the tumour in my shoulder that affected my ability to use my right arm. My radiation therapist called it a "spot-weld." He was middle-aged, peroxide blonde and ponytailed. He had the body of a professional volleyball player and the intonation of a teenage girl. Everything he said was a question.

"Where there's a possibility of collateral damage to your organs, we're going to use electrons? And then, where we need to penetrate the tumour, we'll use photons? I'm going to make some marks on your skin to direct the beams?"

I undressed and lay on the table, and he produced his stencils and a black marker and drew on my skin, like being tattooed by a child. The radiation therapy machine looks like it would be more at home in NASA than a hospital. It's huge and pivots and whirs, and then its big vacant eye zaps your insides. I've named it HAL. I had forty-five seconds of radiation on my shoulder, and the tumour has already shrunk in size, which has given me back most of the mobility in my arm.

I feel ridiculously joyful opening the refrigerator or brushing my hair. I love this body of mine. I'm hoping madly that this upswing of good health continues.

Ruth

Dear Shashi,

I am beginning to understand moment-to-moment living. I take pleasure. I take all of this wondrousness in. As unnatural and bizarre as this all seems to me, my own death has always been inevitable. And I'm not alone. We will all make this journey. I kept on thinking this shouldn't be happening to me, but this is what happens. We die. What counts is how I spend my time now.

It's hard to not to wallow in grief and self-pity, but the cure is absorption in the world and deep engagement with life. I read, I take photos, I kiss Noah, and I go to the pool and float around on my back in the warm water. I think of you on your weekend trip to Nice with Mike, and I picture the blue of the Mediterranean.

And I'm still hopeful. My oncologist thinks we might achieve stasis yet. I do feel better than I have in weeks, and while I'm not in any way in perfect shape, it is encouraging to see my body work at healing itself. Despite the poor scan results, I believe I might actually beat this thing. Melanoma has a high percentage of spontaneous remissions. It's possible my immune system could go into overdrive and destroy the tumours. I read an article about a man whose melanoma had metastasized to his lungs and liver; he went into remission and lived twenty years. I have to believe I could be one of the lucky ones.

Ruth

Dear Shashi,

I finally got all the results from the scans for the Proleukin trial. The tumours beneath my clavicle have all shrunk by a several centimetres. But the tumour next to my sternum is bigger. There's new growth too. The cancer has metastasized to my liver, lungs and into my right bicep. The good news is that the majority of my tumours are still located in my bone and soft tissue, and the tumours I do have in my internal organs are not yet interfering with the essential functioning of my body.

My oncologist prescribed another immune booster called Yervoy, which is currently offered as a treatment option for patients who have not responded well to other therapies. He assured me this is not the medical equivalent of a farewell drink in the Last Chance Saloon, and that I should think of my recent tumour growth, and coming off the Proleukin trial, as a setback and not as the end of the line. The new treatment will begin next week. I have not fully processed all of this information yet and what it truly means for me. I'm not happy, but I'm trying to roll with the punches.

Yours,

Ruth

Dear Shashi,

On Tuesday night, on my walk from the cinema to the car, I collapsed. My body contorted, and I crumpled onto the asphalt. Even with Noah's help, my left leg would not hold me, so he called an ambulance. I had an emergency MRI of my brain and upper-neck, with my head clamped inside a padded cradle. I wore a plastic cage, similar to an ice hockey mask, over my face, and I had to lie perfectly still like that for an hour, inside a tunnel only 24 inches in circumference. I tried not to think of coffins. The honking and clanging of the electric coils was so loud that even with earplugs it sounded as though I were at a construction site. The scan showed a tumour in my brain toward the back of my skull that's swollen and bleeding and the source of my motor dysfunction.

It's probably an understatement to say this has been a challenging development. Forget flying or being invisible. I think standing up might be the best ability. Noah is manly enough to carry me from room to room like a blushing bride, but once he goes to work, I'm in a wheelchair.

While we were out grocery shopping in the canned goods aisle, with Noah alternating between steering me and steering the cart, we bumped into a social worker I knew through the counselling centre.

"Oh my goodness," she said. "I'm so sorry. Have you been in an accident?"

"No," I said. I felt Noah, frozen to the spot behind me, stricken with a can of garbanzo beans in his hand. "I have cancer."

She didn't know where to look, and I felt this terrible shame for my damaged body. No one likes to look at me full on. I'm an aberration. I'm a leper.

We're not sure when I'll be able to walk again. The tumour's location renders it inoperable. The oncologist has me on a drug regimen to reduce the inflammation; Dexamethasone for the swelling, Topamax to ease the nerve pain, Voltarol as a muscle relaxant and a dose of Oxycodone just for good measure. There was an old woman who swallowed a fly.

Yours,

Ruth

Dear Shashi,

My dad arrived last night and looked shocked to see the physical state I am in. I can't accept it either. When I sleep, I dream of a cure being discovered, or of the treatment working or spontaneous remission. I jump out of the wheelchair and go running. I walk back to work, and everyone who knows me stops me on the way, and they all say, "Thank God, Ruth, you look so well, I'm so glad." Sometimes, even in my dreams, I remember it isn't true, and my legs give way, and I keel over onto the sidewalk, or in the middle of all the well-wishing, my phone rings and it's my oncologist, and he says, "The CT scan shows a large tumour in your liver," and I start to sob.

There's a lot of fear in this house. I've assembled the three people in the world who care most if I live or die and have asked them to witness my decline. I know they grieve and suffer. Noah is utilizing all of his flex days, so he's home a lot, and I'm glad for that. He spends most of his time lying in bed with Wingnut and me, giggling and kissing and staring at the sky. Yesterday I lost it because I realized that if I die, he'll meet someone else, and they'll have this life instead of me. I know it's unfair and unreasonable, but I was angry with him that he gets to keep living. I cried, and he stroked my hair and said, "Ruthie, it's not as if I want you to die. You're my person. I want to live my whole life with you."

I don't want to give this up.

Yours,

Ruth

Dear Shashi,

I elected not to continue treatment with Yervoy. The likelihood of recovery is remote, and besides, along with liver failure and perforated intestines, one of the listed side effects of Yervoy is Death. Can death be a side effect? I always thought death took centre stage.

Noah tried to talk me into going to the US or trying different treatment options here in Canada, but it is impossible for either of us to deny the situation I'm now in. I'm beginning to experience shortness of breath because the tumours in my left lung interfere with my ability to get oxygen. I feel as though my chest is full of soggy cotton balls.

My pain is mostly managed, and I dispense my own drugs, which is a full-time job, as my drug regimen is best described as rigorous. Magnesium salts and extended release pills and fentanyl patches and then a serving of haloperidol to stop me vomiting everything back up, followed by a glass of water and a long nap. In some ways, I'm grateful for my drug regimen, as it gives a sense of focus and control to my life. I feel as if I am doing something to cope.

I'm still no closer to knowing when I'll die. My health will deteriorate. The doctors cannot predict how, but they suspect my lungs will continue to be compromised, as that's where my tumour growth has been most rampant in the last few weeks. I'm determined to see as little of the antiseptic insides of the hospital as I can and wring every last bit of living out of my body. It's been relieving to finally opt out of treatment. I've gone rogue. I wish I had done it earlier. Just said no thank you to the toxins and the side effects and the waiting rooms and the roller coaster of scan results. At the time, I thought I was choosing life, but instead, I chose the possibility of a future over the quality of the present. Either way, it's all hindsight wisdom now.

Life is extraordinary and not at all what I thought. I never could have fathomed this. Think of us both riding around in your mom's old Ford Taurus with the windows down, singing to U2 until our throats hurt. If someone had taken me aside then and told me this was coming, I never would have believed them. My life story has been bizarrely truncated. I've swerved off the road. I think of all the plans Noah and I made: weekend camping trips and saving up for a top-of-the-line touring bike and going to the Belle and Sebastian show in Toronto in November, and it pains me so much that sometimes I wish I had never existed at all.

It's difficult for me to accept that I'll never be old, that this is truly what happens to me: I get sick, and I die at age thirty-three. I will be your friend that died young. Underpinning all my living has been the assumption that I would die in my nineties after a full and rich life. But that's a lie. All of us with our clean scrubbed faces live next to a black hole.

Yours,

Ruth

Dear Shashi,

Your care package arrived yesterday. Thank you for the books and the tee-shirt. I'd forgotten all about my teenage love of *Pinky and the Brain*. I wear the shirt all the time.

If I'm going to die at thirty-three, I want to do it with grace and dignity, not as an egotistical monster, but I have to stop myself from yelling at Noah and my parents, "Bring me bonbons now! NOW! I'm dying" or "Change the channel. I hate soccer. I don't care if you like it. Which one of us is dying? Huh?" I want all my whims catered to. I often find myself thinking, Noah should do this for me because he'll have his whole life after my death to do what he wants. But we're all potentially dying. We either owe each other everything all the time, or we owe each other nothing and get to choose what we're able to give to others.

It's a beautiful morning, sunny and crisp, and I'm lying here watching a very fat robin in the plum tree. In this moment, my biggest wish is to live to see summer. I want Noah to take me to the lake so I can lie in the shade and drink lemonade and feel the heat of the sun in the sand against my skin.

Yours,

Ruth

Dear Shashi,

On Monday, my palliative care nurse informed me that we've entered the end stage. Of course, some part of me already knew. This body is not long for the world. A large tumour bulges below my clavicle, and about six more have bloomed across my ribcage. My kidneys ache unrelentingly. The lymph nodes in my left armpit are distended and rubbery. My skin has begun to feel too small for what is now inside it.

But it was so difficult to hear her say that aloud. I'm unfixable. I don't even understand how that's possible. It's astonishing to me that there is no way to reverse this. Isn't there a Mars Rover? Drone attacks? 3D printers? Surely, someone can help me.

I suppose at least there will be no more waiting. My course is set. These last nine months, I've felt as though I were in the path of an unfolding accident, desperately trying to find a way to avoid impact. Now there's nothing left to do but roll into it.

I live my life in daily increments. I push forward into the most reduced of futures. I eat whatever I like, with no concern for my figure, which remains terrifyingly trim, and I watch endless movies. I make Noah choose what to watch because I simply freeze up when I have to make the decision. What if this is the last movie I ever see and it's a dud? I can't take responsibility for that.

So the answer to your question is yes. Come and see me now. I don't think it can be delayed and I want to see your face.

Ruth

Dear Shashi,

I'm glad you enjoyed my celebration of life. I did too. I'm pleased I didn't have to die first in order to attend it. I don't know why everyone doesn't have a pre-death celebration. You ought to be able to eat the finger food and drink the wine. God knows you've paid for it.

In the ten days since you and Mike left for Paris, the doctors informed me that the lining of my left lung has begun to fill with fluid, and my kidneys are threatening to go on strike. I fractured a rib getting into bed. A tumour in my cervical spine has grown so big I have trouble holding up my head. When I'm moved, I feel as though my organs have come loose and slosh against each other. Typing this takes so much effort. Even lifting the phone up to my ear exhausts me. Noah puts me in an armchair by the window, and I stare out at the sky like an oversized tabby cat.

Do you remember how my dad travelled for work so much when I was a kid? I used to go with Mom to take him to the airport sometimes. The divider between the main lobby and the old departure lounge had those wooden panels with windows. The panels didn't go all the way to the floor, so we'd always reach under and touch his hand before he disappeared through the swinging doors and out onto the tarmac. I was full of gratitude for that last touch even though it upset me so much to say good-bye.

Always,

Ruth

Acknowledgements

Thank you to all the early readers of these stories, including Annabel Lyon, Maureen Medved, Kim McCullough, Aaron Counts, Kate Lum and Gail Anderson-Dargatz, and my editor Pearl Luke, for your insights and wisdom.

To Mona Fertig, my publisher, for her generosity and patience. To Mark Hand, for the beautiful cover design.

To my fellow melanoma warriors, who face their illnesses and their mortality with such humour and grace, you continually inspire me.

To Pia Lironi, who upon being told, no, I could not come out to play because I was working on my book, said, "Just end the story with them all getting abducted by aliens."

To my friends and family for their kindness and support, and for believing in me when I informed them age 5 that I would be a writer when I grew up.

This book was finished despite my best friend in the entire world, Shawn Dirksen, who always thought he knew better, even though he's never written a story before in his life.